KC Mills Presents

My Savage Ain't For Everybody 2
By: Jaii Lynn

Acknowledgments

Wow! We are four books in?!

To God be the glory, always and forever.

To my first love Zyion Armani, everything I do is for you baby boy. I pray every night that you are proud to call me your mom just as proud as I am to call you my son.

To my wonderful mother aka NahNah, my secretary, my bff, my crybaby, my backbone, I love you, mommy. I hope you are just as proud of me as I am.

To my Admin Crew, Brittany aka Renae, Denica aka My Nica Boo, Shandrea, Dora Dora The Explorer, Erica The Synopsis Queen and my Trinity, I love all y'all aggy selves! We go through this book struggle together ladies, and I wouldn't want to go through this with any other crew.

To K.C. Mills the best publisher hands down, I thank you for this amazing opportunity.

To BriAnn Danae my inspiration and hometown author, you are the best!

To my pen sister Nikki Brown, you are amazing thank you!

To The Squad, y'all know how we rockin, I love you!

To my brother, my best friend, my son's godfather, my twin Darius aka RemLocc, you know you are my everything. Thank you for being there for me when I wasn't even there for me!

To ALL MY READERS, rather you have been rocking since Captivated, or if you're just now tuning in, from the bottom of my heart, I THANK YOU ALL. Every share, every re-post, every question, every review, every discussion, every like NEVER goes unnoticed! I'm forever grateful for the love and support!

If I left anyone out insert yourself here x_____ Thank you!

- *Jaii Lynn, The Authoress*

Where We Left Out...

Essynce

"Why did you drop him off? You never told me you had a son by one of the Miahgo's." Essynce fired off questions at Nefe as she paced back and forth in Essynce's private hospital room.

"I couldn't risk my job. Having Lyberti would have compromised everything. But I think I fucked up either way." Nefe said.

"Yeah, I'm shocked he let you go after you revealed that to him. So, what are you going to do now?" Essynce asked wincing in pain as she tried to sit up. She had a broken arm and bruises all over, but fortunately for her, the seat belt saved her life. Essynce had passed out due to bumping her head, but other than the broken arm she walked away with little to no serious injuries.

"Honestly I'm just winging this shit. Lyberti is my way in so when I dropped him off at the other entrance I knew he would find his way to Lessiin, now all I have to do is wait it out a little bit." Nefe said as she sat down in the chair next to Essynce's bed.

"I hope you're right. How is Landon? Is all my info secured?" Essynce asked.

"He's still in a coma. They can't divulge any of your info and as far as the Miahgo's they just know that your parents have you in private care until you heal. Don't worry your cover is fine," Nefe explained.

"Okay good," Essynce said before laying her head back pushing the nurse call button; she was ready for her meds, so she could feel better and go back to sleep. Her mind has been racing since the night of the incident. That crazy ass Taliyah had really tried to kill them all. Unfortunately for Landon's opponent, he didn't make it, he died that night on the street.

"Yes?" The mid shift nurse replied.

"May I have something for my pain please?" Essynce asked her, and she nodded her head letting her know she would send someone in to assist her.

While they waited, they heard a page over the intercom placing the hospital on lockdown. That was odd, but whenever the nurse came in, Essynce was going to ask her.

"Ok, Ms. Powell here is your medication. Could you tell me your date of birth please?" The nurses were all so nice on the floor, and very caring and professional. Essynce recited her date of birth, and the nurse scanned her wristband.

*CODE BLUE ICU ROOM 6. CODE BLUE ICU ROOM 6**

The intercom went off again causing Nefe to jump out of the seat. Essynce looked over at her concerned

"That's Landon's room!" Nefe yelled looking at a frightened Essynce.

"Wait noooooooo!" Essynce screamed.

Leylan

Beep Beep Beep

The constant beeping of the heart monitor woke Leylan up out of her sleep. Looking around her surroundings she opened and closed her eyes a few times to adjust to the lighting around the room.

"What the fuck?" Leylan said groggily trying to understand where she was and how she had gotten there. As if a light went off in her head she tried sitting up fast. The last thing she remembered was the doctor saying they tried everything they could.

"Calm down" Leylan whipped her head to the side to see Emory sitting up staring at her.

"Aint no calm down. Where are my brothers?" Leylan sassed.

"I'm gone let you have that since you just woke up after passing out, but you should bring that attitude down a few notches." Emory said in an even tone.

"Look I don't have an attitude, it's a lot going --"

"Oh, auntie your awake, you were sleepy" Lyberti hopped up running towards Leylan's bed trying to climb up.

"Yeah, I was neph, I'm up now. Can you let me talk to Em for a minute and then we can talk some more, ok?" Leylan said softly and Lyberti nodded his little head walking back over to pull out couch in the room and occupied himself with some toys he had.

"Landon is stable, but still in a coma. The doctor explained that his body went into shock for some unknown reason and while they were working on him he did flatline. He was resuscitated, and they have him in a medically induced coma. When they revived him his brain activity heightened, and they just want him to stay under to heal and rest." Emory explained everything causing Leylan to let out the breath she didn't know she was holding.

"Okay, where's Lessiin?" Leylan inquired, actually surprised she didn't wake up to Lessiin's piercing eyes staring at her. Emory put her head down causing Leylan's monitor to speed up.

"Emory look at me! Where is Lessiin? Why isn't he in here?" Leylan fired off question after question.

"Look, Lessiin and Jream got arrested," Emory said

"WHAT?! For what?" Leylan threw the sheet covering her body off and tried standing up. The door opened as soon as both of her feet touched the ground, in walked two nurses.

"Ms. Miahgo, we are happy you are awake. You shouldn't be on your feet though dear." The oldest of the two nurses said.

"I'm discharging myself," Leylan said trying to take the I.V. out of her arm.

"Ok, we do not recommend you doing that before the doctor has examined you." The second younger nurse said.

"I don't care about any recommendations ma'am, I just got upset and passed out. I'm fine, please one of you take this I.V. out before I do. I need to go." Leylan demanded. Her mental state was in shambles as she sat waiting for the nurse to finish up whatever she needed to do.

"Seneca is already down at the precinct Bliss." Emory tried comforting Leylan, but she wasn't hearing it. She was about to cause havoc on the streets and people who didn't want to be affected should steer clear.

"Auntie, can we go see my daddy?" Lyberti asked in a soft voice. Leylan had forgotten about Lyberti that fast.

"Uhm yeah Neph, let me find out somethings Ouch!" The nurse had removed Leylan's I.V. causing her a little unexpected pain.

"Oohh you got a band-aid now!" Lyberti said excitedly causing everyone in the room to chuckle or smile.

"Alright Ms. Miahgo, you are able to discharge yourself now, although we do not recommend it." The older nurse stated hoping she would change her mind, but she obviously didn't know Leylan Miahgo.

Leylan got out the bed and walked over to the bag Emory was holding out towards her and went into the bathroom to change out of the hospital gown. Once she returned to the room, both nurses were gone, and Lyberti and Emory were standing by the door waiting.

"Here's your phone and purse," Leylan nodded her head accepting her belongings. Walking past the nurse's station and straight to the elevator, Leylan waited while her phone came back on.

"Is Jream's car here, or mine?" Leylan asked.

"Seneca had both cars parked at her house, you're riding with me Bliss," Emory said as they got to the powder blue Nissan Maxima. Leylan helped Lyberti inside and hopped in the passenger seat.

"Look Em, I know I have hella explaining to do; but please, please stop calling me Bliss" Leylan begged.

"It's a habit. I'll try my best, but yes missy you owe me a helluva explanation. We've been working together for a few years, and frankly, I'm shocked that your family hasn't caught on. How have you kept this secret so long and why? I mean just from being around you guys, it's pretty obvious that money isn't an issue" Emory had been waiting to have this conversation with Leylan, but this is the first time they had been alone to bring it up.

"I just needed something that didn't involve *them*. Do you know what it's like being a Miahgo? No, you don't. The shit is mad annoying, being at the club gave me that peace. I wasn't Leylan Miahgo, I wasn't part of the deadly trio, I wasn't a well-trained assassin, I was just Bliss; that's all." Leylan spoke while looking out the window.

"Damn," Emory responded at a loss for words. She couldn't relate to Leylan's plight, and she wouldn't lie and say she could. For the rest of the ride to the precinct there was silence, no radio only the sounds of breathing could be heard. Lyberti had fallen asleep in the backseat, and both girl's minds were all over the place with one main thought in mind, their men.

Seneca

"Ms. Miahgo-Burns, this isn't going to be an easy task at all. Both guys were in the vehicle at the time they were arrested. There was a dismembered body in the trunk." The family's attorney explained.

"I get what you are saying, but there must be some type of footage showing that they weren't the ones who put the body there. Lessiin hadn't even left the hospital floor in about a day, and Jream had just gotten there in a totally different vehicle." Seneca explained not believing out of all the damn things her cousins had done in life, this messy shit was what got one of them locked up.

"We will definitely be exhausting all options, this is not going to be easy especially after we find out who that body belonged to. Now the marijuana charge will be easily dismissible. For now, we will focus on getting them a bond and deal with everything else." Mr. Finelley explained. Standing at six-foot-two slim built with coal black hair he kept cut low and slicked back to perfection Mario Finelley had always been on retainer for the Miahgo's for as long as Seneca could remember. Surprisingly they hadn't had to use him for anything, but they knew he was a beast in the courtroom from other peers who they referred to him.

"What time is the bail hearing?" Seneca asked

"In about an hour and a half. It'll be across the street so just meet me over there. I'm going back to talk to the guys and tell them what to expect." Mario said walking away leaving Seneca on the bench they had occupied.

As Seneca was about to get up to go check in with Emory, she saw Rocky walking inside the building. Although now wasn't quite the time to be having the thoughts she was having, Seneca couldn't help but admire her handsome ass husband. At the age of forty-two Rocky didn't look a day over twenty-five in her opinion. An even six feet, two hundred thirty-pound, caramel complected very distinguished man, Rocky was what the young girls called a 'Zaddy.' Seneca got up to meet him halfway and wrapped her arms around his waist resting her head on his chest taking a deep breath.

Seneca was the rock of the Miahgo clan and had always been. Even as a teen she was always so mature for her age and the most dependable. Due to a terrible decision she had made in her early twenties, Seneca was never able to have children of her own, so the joy she got from raising the triplets was all the joy she needed.

"I love you Sen," Rocky told her in a low tone tightening the hold he had on her.

"I love you more," Seneca responded pulling away and looking up at her husband. She needed that twenty seconds of affection because she knew shit was about to get crucial for a while and her hard exterior would have to be on the forefront for the most part.

"Have you talked to my Uncle?" Seneca asked.

"Nah. His phone is still going straight to voicemail. I sent somebody over to his house though to check on some shit, I can't see him being off the grid right now." Rocky said as he turned around and held Seneca's hand leading her out of the precinct.

"Yeah, something is up for sure," Seneca responded before she turned hearing her name being called. She saw Leylan along with Lyberti and Emory and shook her head. She should have known that damn Leylan wasn't going to stay in the hospital long.

"Why are you down here? I know the doctor did not release you." Seneca said concerned.

"And I know you know I wasn't staying laid up when my man and my brother are locked up Sen." Leylan smartly replied.

"Don't start that shit Fat Ma," Rocky said knowing how Seneca and Leylan could get being that were both alpha females they clashed often.

"So, what is Finelley talking about and what the hell happened?" Leylan asked as they all crossed the street. Lyberti had deserted Leylan's grasp and clung to Rocky.

"So, when Lessiin and Jream were in the car something happened and according to what Lessiin had told Finelley when he went and opened the trunk there was a cut up body in the trunk at the same time the boys pulled up, arresting them on the spot," Seneca explained

"Mann what?! Whose body?" Leylan knew it was some shit in the game at this point and she was going to find out what was up.

"They haven't identified it as of yet. Right now, we are waiting on their charges to be read and see if they get a bond." Seneca further explained to everyone as they huddled closely watching the clock tick with so much on their minds.

Essynce

"You need to calm down before they lock your ass up!" Nefe said between gritted teeth as she watched Essynce start hyperventilating and carrying on.

"Don't tell me to calm down! We both know what Code Blue means, and I'm not a heartless bitch such as yourself!"

"But you are the law! You done sat here and fell in love with your case little girl, I knew your weak ass wasn't going to be able to do this." Nefe fussed pulling out her phone.

"Who are you calling?" Essynce yelled trying her hardest to get herself together.

"The boss! You need to get off this case before you fuck everything up" Nefe replied smartly.

"No! I'm fine, I mean what the fuck do you expect? I've been with this man for some months daily, and we both just had a terrible accident. Come on you couldn't be that heartless to not understand Nefe!" Essynce pleaded.

"Alright, alright, look kid calm down okay. I will find out what's going on and keep you in the loop. Until you have healed, nobody but us and your immediate family will know where you are." Nefe explained to Essynce that she would be getting transferred out of the current hospital because they couldn't risk the chances of any Miahgo's or affiliates catchin' wind of her identity.

"Let me find out how long the transfer will be, I'll be back." Nefe stepped out of the room, and Essynce head fell back. Hoping that the tightness from her eyes being shut would hold the tears that were dying to bust through, was an epic fail. Her cheeks were covered in wetness, and if she hadn't taken her uninjured hand and clamped it over her mouth, the whole hospital floor would of her heard her wailing.

As ironic as it may sound with Essynce trying to play the role of taking down the Miahgo's, she never wanted him to die. She would be a full-blown liar if she said she hadn't developed feelings for Landon in the short period they had been together. Her heart was so heavy with the thoughts of Landon actually being dead, she couldn't take it. She knew she would have to put on this brave front in front of everyone, but every moment she was alone, she would be breaking down. Wiping her tear stained face just as Nefe walked back into the room holding her phone to her ear with a serious expression on her face.

Essynce remained silent until Nefe completed her call.

"Lessiin's been arrested." Nefe sat down defeated

"Huh? What? How? What is the deal with this family?" Essynce asked with the feeling in her stomach that things were about to get turned up quick.

Loyal

"So, you mean to tell me, they are all hittas?" Loyal asked knowing he heard it right the first time.

"Dude, hittas ain't got shit on these triplets, they are the coldest set of assassins from the Midwest. How did you not know you were related to them?" Rumi asked. Rumi once a Kansas City native had moved out to California after serving a bid that started at the age of sixteen. Rumi and Loyal had been sick with the computer skills for as long as they could remember, and those tech-savvy ways are what landed Rumi in prison.

After serving his time, Rumi relocated to California where he opened quite a few restaurants. Still not shy to computer works, when Loyal called him for help he jumped on it.

"You forgot my folks ain't shit?" Loyal asked with his face turned up in a scowl thinking about Laila and Dimengo.

"I mean no, how could I forget? But I'm saying, the Miahgo's run the town and you are a Miahgo. I just figured you would have put two and two together." Rumi said still shocked that his best friend was in fact related to the infamous assassins.

"I never heard the name until I start digging. But check this out, Dimengo wants me to tap into all their accounts and give him the codes so he can clean them out. That's why I called you; I need you to make four or five dummy accounts for me." Loyal asked knowing Rumi could do it with little to no effort.

"That's it? I thought you really needed me to dust off the gloves." Rumi joked "I'll have that for you in twenty-four hours brody." He assured.

"Good look. Aye me and Jersey are coming out there for Valentine's day, so get ready." Loyal told him before they exchanged a few more words before disconnecting the call.

Loyal already had his mind made up the day he met with Dimengo that he would die before he helped his bitch ass sperm donor. Dimengo thought he was slick and some of the shit he talked sounded all fine and dandy, but what he forgot was that although Loyal didn't grow up with the rest of his siblings, he still inherited that savage trait that all Miahgo's seemed to own.

Getting up and walking out of the room, he went to the second bedroom turned office space and shut the door, he saw it was going on 12:15 and if his timing was correct, Jersey would be walking in the door in about three minutes. Heading to the bathroom to handle his business, Loyal finished up and went to wash his hands. He heard the beeping from the door opening, and he knew Jersey was now home.

Walking into the living room he stood in the doorway watching her try to be quiet as she stepped out of her work shoes. The house was quiet as it normally was when she got home so not thinking Loyal was up she sat her bags down quietly on the couch. Finally looking up, she yelped startled at a grinning Loyal standing there.

"You could have made some noise bae damn! I almost peed on myself!" Jersey fussed as Loyal eyed her frame that couldn't help but show in the thin pink scrubs that adorned her body.

"You know you the only noisemaker around here. How was your day baby?" Loyal asked while walking over and bending down to wrap his arms around her waist. Kissing her softly a few times before he allowed her to answer, Jersey wrapped her arms around his neck.

"Just a normal day, well it was a little wild but cool for the most part," Jersey said gazing into Loyal's eyes. One thing about the both of them, they loved each other's presence. They could sit around each other daily and one never getting on the other's nerves. It was like they were in sync, as one. Jersey always looked at Loyal with the same love rather it was in the heat of a spat they may have been having or just a good morning.

"Why wild, what happened?" Loyal asked, genuinely interested. He really liked hearing the stories Jersey would tell about what was going on at the hospital she worked at.

"What you eat? Come in the shower with me, and I'll tell you about my wild day." Jersey said while pulling Loyal by his hand down the short hallway that led to their bathroom.

"I ate a sandwich earlier. I'm not getting in that lava shower with your ass either Jersey! I'll sit on the toilet or whatever but on my mama, you not giving me second degree burns tonight." Loyal fussed serious as a heart attack. He never understood why women had to have no cold water at all in their showers, but tonight he wasn't going for it.

Jersey bent over laughing at the serious expression on Loyal's face and shook her head trying to calm herself down. She turned to turn the shower on, so it could warm up while she undressed. Loyal, just as mannish as he wanted to be stood there eyeing her lustfully thinking of all the freaky positions he could twist her in. Jersey was into gymnastics as a kid, so her legs were like noodles, and Loyal took full advantage every chance he got.

"Naw stop slobbering, you don't want to get in the shower with me, so I won't be showering you." Jersey teased licking her tongue out and pulled the shower curtain back stepping into the steamy shower.

"I bet I get showered and it won't be by that lava shower you got going on behind that curtain." Loyal joked.

"So anyway! These dudes got arrested in the parking lot, like they had the whole hospital on lockdown, I heard they found a body or something in the trunk. Then do you remember the car wreck guy I told you about?" Jersey asked

"Yeah, the crazy bitch hit him. What about him?" Loyal asked still thinking about the body situation.

"Well he died, but they were able to save him, and now he has a little more brain activity than before," Jersey explained as she ended her shower and stepped out dripping wet.

"Pass me my towel freak." Jersey joked as Loyal held it above his six-foot-three frame teasing her. Boldly grabbing at his crotch on reflex Loyal had to lower his hands to guard himself helping Jersey gain better leverage for her towel.

"I win!" She teased squeezing past Loyal heading to their bedroom.

"You're a midget ass cheater bruh." Loyal stalked behind her unwrapping the towel from her body. Jersey lowered her eyes biting her bottom lip as Loyal's hands started to roam all over her naked body.

"I missed you bae," Loyal said lowly planting small kisses on her neck trailing to her collarbone leading them down to her chest. When he kneeled down on one knee and latched on to Jersey's perky Hershey kissed shaped nipple, he heard her gasp. Taking one hand, he started rubbing on her inner thighs still not letting up on the tongue lashing he was giving her nipple. Jersey's breathing started to hitch as his hand made its way up her thick thigh and to her hidden treasure.

Stroking her clit slowly with his pointer and middle finger, Loyal stood up and softly pushed Jersey back towards the bed. Not missing a beat Jersey spread her legs as far as they could go while Loyal continued his assault on her clit. Diving head first Loyal latched onto Jersey's swollen clit and started humming the ABC's sending her into a frenzy.

"Ooohh bae you so fucking nasty! That feels so good!" Jersey moaned out winding her hips riding the wave of ecstasy that was shooting through her soul.

"I'm ready for that shower now ma." Loyal said into her pussy as he licked up and down her opening dipping his tongue in and out. Loyal certified himself as a head doctor, so he knew exactly what to do to get the results he needed from Jersey.

Pinning her thighs back making her knees touch her forehead Loyal dipped low sticking his tongue deep into her hot wet tunnel, Jersey's moans were muffled due to the position she was locked in, but he got the point. Taking his free hand Loyal inserted two fingers into Jersey slowly and latched on to her clit at the same time. Jersey started bucking at the simultaneous action that was taking place, and all it took was Loyal spelling his name on her clit with his warm tongue to have Jersey coming in seconds. Breathing hard, Loyal felt her legs become weak and let them down softly while trailing kisses up from her hip to her stomach to the middle of her breast until he reached her soft lips. Jersey stuck her tongue in Loyal's mouth savoring her own juices while reaching down pulling his dick out of his basketball shorts.

Loyal was rock hard and ready, he grabbed Jersey by her waist lifting her up before lying flat on the bed. Jersey mounted him in anticipation. Slowly sliding down his ten-inch pole, after all this time Jersey still had to get used to his size. Tightening her muscles as she sat all the way down.

"Sssssss, damn ma" Loyal hissed out once Jersey hit bottom. Jersey started winding her hips like an island girl making Loyal deeper than he already was. The friction on her clit was causing her to start leaking which was driving Loyal crazy, grabbing her hips with both hands Loyal lifted Jersey up and pulled her back down at a steady pace.

Jersey saw Loyal's eyes start to get low, so she knew this was her chance, taking her leg and swinging it over Jersey flipped around to the reverse cowgirl position without missing a beat and causing Loyal's muscles in his stomach to tighten up.

"Awwhh fuck I feel you bae," Loyal moaned out.

Jersey took that as her cue, as the beat to Trina's '*Look Back at Me*" started playing in her own head Jersey took off on the dick showing no mercy. Loyal was gripping and trying to keep up, and Jersey kept up her pace throwing a dirty wind in every now and then. Once Jersey had cum two more times she felt Loyal's dick start to pulsate, so she knew he was close.

Jersey planted both feet flat on the bed and got in froggy hop position tightening her walls as best she could she bounced about four times before she heard Loyal let off an animalistic roar indicating that she had drained all the life out of him. Legs too numb for her to get up Jersey fell forward not moving for a while.

As the two started to regulate their breathing, Loyal popped Jersey on her round ass making her huff.

"Bae that was that deal, what song was you riding to ma?" Loyal had to know.

"My bitch Trina of course," Jersey said in funny tone while making her ass shake while she still laid flat on her stomach. Loyal headed to the bathroom to get cleaned up and get a rag to clean Jersey's noodle leg ass up.

"Open up." Loyal coached a sleeping Jersey as he cleaned her up with the warm soapy towel he had brought out for her. He knew she would be knocked out after working her shift and putting down that show so he softly rolled her over and through the fleece blanket she couldn't sleep without on her body before going out to the living room to smoke.

Loyal had to check on some of the kids he mentored tomorrow, so he knew he needed to be going to bed soon. Firing up the backwood blunt he looked over to see the time that illuminated from the cable box. It was going on three am, so after a few hits of the blunt Loyal put it out in the ashtray before joining his love in the bed.

"I love you LoLo" Jersey mumbled, cuddling up under him

"I love you too ma," Loyal returned with a soft kiss on her forehead as the two drifted off to sleep.

Lessiin

"Miahgo and Sirtain! Miahgo! Sirtain! Let's go your bond has been posted!" The loud officer yelled for no reason at all. There was a hand full of muthafuckas in the holding tank, so there was no reason to be yelling.

The look of pure irritation had been painted on Lessiin's face since they were handcuffed and brought in. Even during the intense interrogation, Lessiin never offered an alternative expression.

"One two-step gentleman, unless you want to stay!" The obnoxious guard smartly remarked.

"Is all that necessary, damn its ten niggas up in here, and this shit is the size of a shoe box, the fuck you yelling for?" Jream irritably snapped causing the officer to clamp his mouth shut. Having been working in the booking department of the Kansas City Police department for over twelve years, the officers learned who to fuck with and not. Lessiin and Jream definitely fit the bill of the not to be fucked with crew. Nothing else could be heard as the trio made their way up to the desk to complete the process.

Lessiin didn't give a fuck about a thing they were telling him as far as his rules for bond. He had shit to fuck up streets to paint red, and as far he was concerned the muthafucka holding him up could add to the paint job.

"Did you get that Mr. Miahgo, did you hear me?" The officer asked getting an uneasy feeling in his stomach for some odd reason. But he was right, Lessiin was milliseconds from snapping if he didn't walk up out of there soon.

Nodding his head slowly and giving the officer one of the coldest looks, he shifted his weight about to open his mouth when he heard a familiar voice. Turning his head in the direction he heard the voice coming, his eyes connected with the prosecuting attorney. A sinister smile spread across his face, locking eyes with Malia Rose.

Normally a 'Pitbull in a skirt' in the courtroom, Malia Rose was the definition of don't judge a book by its cover. Light brown complexion oozed over her petite frame, high cheekbones with chinky hazel eyes that sat cased behind her Armani frames. Malia was far from a video vixen, but she held her own in a room full of bad bitches.

"What's up Rosie?" Lessiin said in a cool demeanor, he could smell the fear oozing from Malia and that's what he thrived off of.

"H-He-Hello Mr. Miahgo," Malia said trying to regain some type of composure

"Well, you know. I'll be seeing you soon Rosie" Lessiin said with another nod of his head and turning to follow Jream and the officer out of the facility.

Before Rosie had 'changed for the better,' she was living a life of destruction, your typical hood tale; one single parent household, unruly teenage girl, doing whatever to get by to try and find her way. One night, in particular, woke young Malia Rose up, what went from a normal Saturday night party, turned into Malia being kidnapped and she and her best friend Monique repeatedly gang-raped. Her best friend was killed right in front of her very own eyes and a week after being held beyond her will Malia's unconscious body was dropped off in a field to die.

That night Malia was found by the training Miahgo triplets and nursed back to health with the help of Cesare. Malia's mother had checked out in the week she went missing and when Monique's body popped up floating in the Missouri river before Malia was found caused her to totally lose it. Malia's mother hopped in her car and hit the highway never looking back.

The weeks to come, Malia started healing mind body and soul and decided she was ready to live a better life. She could have met the same fate as Monique, but she felt that God spared her for a reason. With the help of Cesare, Malia continued her education going on to get her degree and becoming the prosecuting attorney for the City of Kansas City, Missouri.

Seeing Lessiin, it wasn't that she was scared of him, but she knew that she was going to end up having to compromise her positioned that she had worked so hard for. She owed the Miahgo's, and she knew that. If it wasn't for that family, there's no telling where she would be right now.

When Lessiin and Jream stepped out of jail they were met by their family; Seneca, Rocky, Leylan, Emory, Romeo, and Lyberti stood posted against the cars they arrived in waiting for their men to come out.

The first one to react was little Lyberti. Although only spending about an hour and a half with his father, his young mind had formed a bond. Lyberti ran up to Lessiin making him crack a small smile as he bent down to pick him up.

"Pops, you good?" Lyberti asked.

"Yeah boy. Ya pops a G," Lessiin assured him amused by his concern.

"What's a G? Can I be a G too?" Lyberti asked innocently making Lessiin chuckle and rub his hand on the young boy's head.

"Right now, you're a young bull, aight? When you get older, you can be a G like me, aight?' Lessiin reasoned with him as his eyes lit up shaking his little head.

"Come on little boy," Seneca said shaking her head and laughing at the exchange between the two. Lessiin put Lyberti down as he ran over to Rocky.

"Damn Fat Ma you all over nightmare over there, fuck ya, brother, huh?" Lessiin joked

"Nigga go feel on Em and let me be, I know you good I felt you the whole time" Leylan responded referencing the triplet bond they all shared.

"Come here ma," Lessiin said motioning for Emory to walk towards him and she complied.

"Don't act like you missed the kid." Emory joked. Lessiin didn't say anything, he just stared at her observing her aura. Lessiin knew before all this shit popped off that he was growing deep feelings for Emory but to see she never left his side when he was just being him while Landon was in the hospital and she was still standing strong amongst his family really did something to him.

Lessiin had the feeling he had found the one but as time went on and shit started to get even more real would be the test. If Emory was still standing once the dust settled, he would know for sure.

"I see you still around these parts, that's a good look ma. Look like them hips spread while I was away too." Lessiin said speaking what was on his mind. Standing clad in white V-neck shirt, a black fleece North Face jacket with mustard yellow leggings and black Ugg boots. Emory was as basic as it could get but to Lessiin she was the baddest bitch in Kansas City right then and there.

"It's only been three days fresh ass. But my ass still fat though." Emory teased wrapping her arms around his waist allowing him to hold her. This moment was good, and all but Lessiin was ready to get down to business.

"We will meet in the morning, seven o'clock." Seneca said reading Lessiin's mind.

As everyone went their separate ways to get in their cars, Lessiin called out to Leylan

"Yom! Three the hard way" Lessiin stated simply, and Leylan walked over to him never breaking eye contact.

"Three the hard way. See you in a minute." Leylan said hugging her brother tightly. They communicated with their eyes and separated heading to the cars. Emory was strapping Lyberti in and holding some kind of conversation with him while Lessiin sat in the driver's seat watching them interact in the rearview.

"How the fuck do you drive this close to the windshield?" Lessiin fussed adjusting the seat to his comfort.

"Well I'm five four and not seven feet so what you think?" Emory sassed while putting her seatbelt on.

"Where y'all been staying?" Lessiin asked pulling out on the practically empty street.

"Home," Emory said with a smirk.

"I see we gone have to get you some act right, but don't worry I'm gone learn you something," Lessiin said smartly.

"Mmmm, I'll be there for that lesson, Lessiin." Emory winked turning to see Lyberti had fallen asleep already.

"What he like?' Lessiin asked

"He his daddy son," Emory said causing both of them to burst out laughing.

"He is so smart and protective. When we went to get some food, so I could cook, a young nigga tried to shoot his shot and he kindly told him in true Lessiin fashion that his 'pops don't play that shit' the little nigga dapped his little ass up and walked smooth off." Emory was red from laughing at the memory.

"Say word? Yo, that little nigga can rock with me." Lessiin was having a proud father moment for sure. In the small amount of time that he had to sit while in holding he thought about what kind of father he could be Lyberti. He didn't know what he was doing in the least bit, but something told him he could do it and do it well.

"Word. My baby is with all the shits." Emory said, after four days she had fallen completely in love with Lyberti. She never entertained the thought of having her own children but after stepping up to a motherly role and knocking it out the park was giving her baby fever for sure.

"We not gone be up here long," Lessiin said as they pulled into the hospital parking lot followed by Leylan and Jream. Lessiin wouldn't dare go home and get comfortable without checking on his brother. Clearly Leylan felt the same way.

No words were spoken as everyone loaded onto the elevator with one thought in mind, Landon.

Walking up to their personal security who stood guard outside Landon's door twenty-four seven. He nodded his head and slapped fives with Lyberti. Lessiin shook his head observing how everyone had excepted his son quickly and Lyberti the same.

Walking in the room everyone's jaw hit the floor.

"Landon!!" Leylan screeched seeing Landon blinking and looking around.

"Let me go get the doctor" Emory rushed out to get help.

"Say, my nigga, what's the deal? You rested?" Lessiin asked keeping his brother attention.

"Landon continued to blink while trying to point at the dry erase board that hung on the wall. Jream saw his gesture and went to grab a pencil and paper. Grabbing something hard to put the paper on Jream got close putting the pencil in Landon's hand, it took a little getting used to, but Landon started to scribble something on the paper.

When he was done, he dropped the pencil closing his eyes.

"Aye yo! Landon wake up bruh; we just got here, you still sleepy nigga?" Lessiin asked feeling a tightness in his chest.

"His monitor is still steady, just wait bruh," Jream coached, handing the paper over to Lessiin and Leylan. They stood side by side trying to read over what their brother had told them.

One more Miahgo. Laila kill me. Nefe fed. 3.

Leylan's once brown eyes had turned coal black. Lessiin's face had contorted to that of an animal. Their blood had run cold reading the note Landon had left them. Just as the door swung, open Leylan had produced her gun on reflex causing the nurse to screech in fear and run back out of the room.

"Aye man!" Jream rushed over to Leylan grabbing her arm and lowering the gun taking it from her. "You know better ma, now is not the time to be reckless baby, now is the time to get your head in the game. What did Landon say?"

With shaking hands, Leylan handed the paper over to Jream so he could read it. It only took about thirty seconds, and Jream looked over at Landon when he finished.

"One more Miahgo? What does that mean?" Jream asked the exact question that question that was on Lessiin's mind.

"That bitch !!!" Leylan screamed out "When Landon started going into shock she was in this room, she was trying to kill him then."

"What?!" Lessiin raised his voice startling Lyberti.

"It was so much going on when you and Jream left to go smoke, and we came back up from the cafeteria Laila's dog ass was up here standing next to Landon's bed with tears coming down her face. When Emory made it inside with Lyberti, I had already drawn down on Laila because I had that feeling and then Lyberti yelled out granny. At that point I was lost as fuck and then Landon's monitor started crashing and all hell broke loose."

"Granny? Lyberti, come here man. Was your granny here?" Lessiin questioned knowing that kids told nothing but the truth most of the time.

"Yes, GranGran was here, Aunt Ley yelled at her to get out! If Aunt Ley doesn't like GranGran, I don't like her either." Lyberti said with assertiveness

"How do you know GranGran and not me?" Lessiin probed further

"Mommy and GranGran always go eat at this nasty place that sells fish," Lyberti said turning his nose up. Lessiin just nodded his head putting pieces to the puzzle together.

"Excuse me, I was told there was a gun in here" A tall skinny guy who must have been hospital security said as he stepped into the room.

"Any gun in here is registered." Lessiin barked, and the security jumped slightly

"O-ok just checking. Is everything alright in here?" The security asked.

"Yeah man damn!" Lessiin barked again.

"Alright." Was all the security guard offered as he scurried out of the room. He was weak and clearly wasn't in the right line of work.

"Hello, I'm doctor Oswald. I heard our patient is awake now." Dr. Oswald said as he walked over to Landon's machines jotting down notes and reading different things.

"Why did he go back to sleep so fast?" Leylan asked wanting to make sure everything was alright with her brother.

"That's normal, from the read I'm getting from his monitors he is just fine, just needs more rest. We will unhook him from the breathing machine because it looks like Landon here is breathing on his own. Once his body feels stronger, he will wake up for longer periods of time. Any wounds he may have, have been healing magnificently as well." Dr. Oswald assured them. As he was leaving, he let them know he was sending a nurse in to remove the breathing and feeding tubes.

About an hour later, Landon had woken up a couple more times for ten-minute intervals but they were more than pleased with that. Gathering their things to leave there was another knock on the door. Everyone was on alert as Emory held Liberty's hand a little tighter pulling him behind her.

"Who are you?" Lessiin and Landon said simultaneously as a tall brown skin guy came fully into the room.

"Aye Lessiin you got some more kids out here?" Jream asked causing Leylan to elbow him lightly. But she had to admit whoever this guy was looked just like Lessiin in his teens.

"How y'all doing? I'm looking for Lessiin, Landon and Leylan Miahgo. I was told Landon was a patient here and got directed to this room." The guy said never breaking eye contact with anyone in the room.

"Who sent you?" Leylan said in a growl while clutching her pistol in the rear of her back ready to lay the young nigga out.

"I'm Loyal."

"That's all fine and dandy but who are you and why are you here?" Lessiin asked. My name is Loyal. Loyal Miahgo. We need to rap." Loyal stated really taking a look around the room observing everyone. When Lessiin opened his mouth to say something they heard coughing coming from behind them.

"You alright?" Lessiin asked Landon as he grabbed the cup trying to give him some water. Landon nodded his head lightly and looked around.

"You got another kid bro?" Landon asked weakly causing laughs to fill the air. Even in his weakest state, Landon was forever a jokester.

"Nigga fuck you! This our brother I'm assuming. Right kid? That's what you wanted to rap about right?" Lessiin asked already figuring that Loyal was of no threat to them.

"Yeah, and some other shit," Loyal said.

"I need a blunt," Leylan complained finally taking her hand off her gun.

"I got you baby." Jream assured with a smirk.

"Aye nightmare, get fucked up lil nigga!" Lessiin fussed while Landon tried to laugh, but ended up having a coughing fit.

"Loyal, I'm your big sister Leyland. The big bad wolf right there is Lessiin and the invalid over in the bed is Landon as you probably already know. The little soldier over there shooting daggers your way is your nephew Lyberti and the hot mama holding him back is Emory also Lessiin's woman. This mediator is Jream. Everyone in here is family. I'm dope as fuck at reading people and what I get from you is all legit." Leylan said looking him and down.

"Come on Ms. Cleo, I'm tired and need a real shower," Jream said grabbing Leylan hand to pull her towards the door.

"We gone rap alright? Tomorrow morning at 7:45 there's a family meeting. I want to hear everything then." Lessiin instructed giving Loyal the address and grabbing Lyberti and Emory walking out the hospital room.

"Yo Loyal," Landon said lowly, making Loyal walk closer to the bed so he could hear him better.

"I can tell you legit too. Just remember, we Miahgo's and we rock with each other the hard way lil nigga." With that being said, Landon laid on his back and closed his eyes he knew Loyal had read between the lines and understood him quite well.

Laila

"Bitch, you must like my foot off in your ass! What the fuck happened?" Dimengo yelled standing over a cowering Laila. He rained punches all over any part of her body that he could.

"I tried!!!" Laila screamed out

"Shut up bitch! You froze up like I knew you would. You love them muthafuckas more than you love me? Huh?!" Dimengo screamed out lifting his foot bringing it down with force.

"No! No! One of them walked in, and I was outnumbered. I swear I was about to suffocate him!" Laila begged hoping this beating would be coming to an end soon. As if God heard Laila's pleas, everything stopped. When she removed her arms from the protective stance she was in; she saw that Dimengo had taken a seat at the table and started on his nose candy.

"Lai listen and listen good because you fucked up, I had to make a move. Laila if you ever think about leaving me you will take your last breath right where you stand. I feel a change in you, when I used to have to get you in line you wanted to do anything in your power to please me, now you just take whatever is coming and move around. I don't like that shit, Lai." Dimengo snorted two lines before continuing, he had made up in his mind that in order to keep Laila in line he had had to keep her low.

"Get up and come hit this. Like I was saying, I knew you would fuck up and not get that job done. So, I used the time you were taking in there doing who the fuck knows what and made the first play. Let me ask you a question Laila; Why don't you want to get rid of them?" Dimengo asked in all seriousness

"They are our children," Laila said as the drugs started to surge through her body, the beating she had just received was nothing to her right now. That was Laila's problem, she was easily distracted and easily manipulated.

"Our children? Mine too?" Dimengo asked, and Laila nodded her head quickly.

"Is there anything you wouldn't do for *your* parents Laila? I say that to say this, our so-called children betrayed us. They knew we were having rough times and we were struggling and everything we did was to help them. So now they are in the position to help us, and they have the nerve to hate us?! All four of them! Yet, you don't want to be down with my plan? That's what pisses me off, Lai! It's always been you and I against the world, but I feel like you are trying to break our union."

"No! I'm not Dimengo, I swear I'm not!" Laila had allowed Dimengo's words to actually make sense to her fragile mind.

"Well, I did what I had to do for our union Laila," Dimengo said not ready to divulge what actions he had really taken.

"While I was at the hospital and Landon flatlined, I saw Lyberti. He is going to be a problem." Laila warned.

"We don't have problems Lai, that's what I'm saying. When did you start doubting me? Have I ever left you without? Huh?" Dimengo asked in a low tone

"N-n-no" Laila shook her head at the same time

"Get Nefe over here so we can wrap some shit up. Laila, I need you to always remember it's me and you until your last breath. Is that understood?" Dimengo asked getting up and clearing the table.

Laila sat there for a while after she heard the shower start and let all of Dimengo's words sink in. Did her kids deceive her and leave her when she was only trying to do what was best for them? Was Dimengo the only one truly in her corner? Those were only a few questions that really stuck out to Laila. Getting up from the table to go get her cell phone, Laila noticed Dimengo's cell phone on the floor, he must have dropped it while he was 'getting her in line.' Not up for any more disciplinary action tonight she left it right where it was.

Making it to the bedroom, Laila picked her phone up and dialed Nefe's number that she had memorized.

"Hello?" Nefe answered quickly.

"We need to meet as soon as possible," Laila said getting right to the point, they both knew the other, so there was no need for introductions and pleasantries.

"Tomorrow 4 pm," Nefe said and disconnected the call right after.

Laila plugged her phone up to the charger and sat on the bed slowly to ease the pain she was feeling all over her body. The drugs were starting to wear off, so she would soon be feeling the effect of Dimengo's wrath.

"Did you call Nefe?" Dimengo asked busting out of the bathroom door.

"Yes, she said tomorrow 4 pm," Laila said.

"Good, good. I'm about to go handle some business are you riding with me or no?" Dimengo asked causing Laila's eyes to pop open in surprise. Dimengo hardly ever invited her anywhere with him anymore, so she was going to take him up on his offer today. Moving as fast as her aching body would allow, Laila went into the bathroom to take a quick shower and clean herself up as much as possible.

Stepping out of the shower Laila got a chance to get a good look at herself. She didn't recognize the reflection staring back at her. The worry lines looked like a never-ending roadmap, the dark rings under eyes were just as bad. The saying 'Black Don't Crack' had definitely missed this one. Laila hurried and finished up in the bathroom not wanting to look at herself much longer. By the time he made it back in the bedroom, Dimengo was fully dressed waiting on her, so she put a pep in her step and got dressed in record timing not wanting to give him a reason to be agitated and leave her.

"You see my phone, Lai?" Dimengo asked as he picked up the car keys and walked towards the door looking around.

"It's over there on the floor by the little couch." Laila pointed out opening the front door. Dimengo went over picking it up. Just as the couple made it out to the car, they both noticed a note on the window on the car. Laila picked it up and opened it, after reading the words she started looking around frightened.

"What is that Laila and the fuck you scared for?" Dimengo barked walking up to her and snatching the note out of her hand. After reading what it said Dimengo crumpled the paper up and walked to the other side of the car and hoped in starting it.

"We got to move quickly." Was all Dimengo said as he pulled out the parking space speeding down the street. Laila had yet to say a word, inside she was scared shitless.

A Lessiin in death is vastly approaching…
The words kept ringing in Laila's head.

Emory

"He really made me lay in that damn bed until he fell asleep" Lessiin fussed.

"He's used to sleeping in here, that's why," Emory said as she sat on the edge of the bed putting lotion all over her freshly showered body.

"You been sleeping with that little nigga?" Lessiin asked with a hint of jealousy regarding his own son. Emory stopped what she was doing and looked at Lessiin to gauge his seriousness and busted out laughing

"Let me find out you're jealous of a four-year-old Mr. Miahgo." Emory joked standing up naked as the day she was born. She sashayed over to a mugging Lessiin and stood on her tippy toes placing soft kisses starting at his collarbone leading up to his chin then his full lips.

Lessiin's face remained stone, but all the blood in his body was rushing to his member down below. Emory and Lessiin had never been sexually involved in the amount of time they had been around each other but tonight seemed like a great opportunity. Lessiin let out a deep breath before bending down and picking Emory up by her thick thighs.

Walking her over to the bed he laid her down on the pillowtop mattress before he pulled his basketball shorts down and kicked them to the side. Now they both were naked, and the fire brewing between the two was enough to spark a house fire.

Emory sat up and grabbed Lessiin's fully erect dick before she started stroking it softly. Lessiin stood still and allowed her to take over for the time being. Emory stroked him softly amazed by his length and thickness. Her mouth watered in anticipation as she leaned forward slightly placing two wet kisses on the head of his member. Finally warming up to him Emory put the tip of his dick on her warm tongue before making a slurping sound and taking in as much as she could.

The quickness caused Lessiin to take a deep breath as her mouth got extra wet and she bobbed up and down on his thickness. Emory suctioned her cheeks around him and continued bobbing dropping slobber in her movements which were driving Lessiin crazy. Taking one of her hands, she grabbed his hanging sack and began massaging it slowly. Lessiin started making a pumping motion in and out of her warm wet mouth, and the sounds coming from Emory's throat was about to make him bust prematurely, so he pulled out roughly.

Eyeing her evilly Emory could read Lessiin like a book, so no words were exchanged when she leaned back sexily and trailed her hands over her perky D cup breasts and trailed them down to her already warm center. Emory took two of her fingers and circled her clit while arching her back pleasing herself and Lessiin. With those same two fingers, she dipped them inside of herself and flicked her wrist slowly causing a moan to escape her lips.

Lessiin had had enough of her teasing ass and decided it was his turn to take over the show. Stepping in-between her already gaped legs, Lessiin stroked himself slowly as he prepared to enter her glistening opening. Pushing her hand out of his way Lessiin pushed all eleven inches inside of Emory with no warning causing her to moan out in pain and ecstasy combined.

"Nah, you wanted to play, so let's play," Lessiin warned as he started his own rhythm between her thighs. Emory was trying to keep up but the death stroke Lessiin was blessing her with had her ready to wave the white flag as he grinded his manhood deep within her.

"Oh my God," Emory moaned out as an orgasm ripped through her body

"It ain't God baby," Lessiin cockily replied as he turned her body roughly positioning her face down and ass up. Once he had her right where he wanted her, he plunged right back in not missing a beat. Grabbing Emory by her hair, he pulled her head back and started sucking roughly on her neck.

"Damn she is talking nasty huh?" Lessiin said lowly in Emory's ear as the sopping sounds of their sex filled the room

"Baby it feels so good, I'm gone cum again," Emory said winding her hips causing Lessiin to hit her spot repeatedly.

"I know" was all Lessiin offered as he let her hair go grabbing her thick hips and drilling into her center. Feeling her knees buckle from under them Lessiin started stroking harder about to reach his climax as well, Emory tightened her walls around him, and the sounds that escaped Lessiin's soul probably woke up everybody in a twenty-mile radius.

Collapsing on top of her Lessiin, tried to gain control of her breathing and Emory was so spent, she didn't know which way was up. After about five minutes Lessiin pulled himself up and out of her and walked away to the bathroom.

Emory rolled to her side of the bed she had claimed and curled up wanting to place her thumb in her mouth, but she was too weak to even move that much. Hearing footsteps, Emory just assumed it was Lessiin coming back in the room until she heard the little voice at the door.

"We got a dog now?" Lyberti asked, causing Emory to throw the sheet over her naked body. He hadn't come into the room, but she wanted to be cautious.

"Umm no baby, why do you ask?" Emory asked sweetly and confused.

"I heard growling," Lyberti said. Emory covered her mouth turning red with embarrassment.

"What you doing up?" She heard Lessiin asking.

"I thought it was a dog in the house," Lyberti explained to his father.

"Na that was Emory snoring, she tired." Lessiin joked opening the bedroom door. Emory had laid back down, so it really looked like she had been sleeping and that was enough for Lyberti, he nodded his head and headed back down the hall to the room he had claimed as his own.

"You sho' right for that lie, dog boy," Emory said tossing a pillow at Lessiin as he got closer to the bed. Shrugging his shoulders, he laid down handing Emory a wet towel.

"Oh, how sweet, but I'm going to take a shower." Emory tried standing up and quickly collapsed back on the bed causing Lessiin to fall over in laughter. This was the first time Emory had ever seen him genuinely laugh, although, at her expense, she still admired his well-defined features.

Trying again Emory was successful this time at keeping her balance.

"You need help Bambi, I mean Em," Lessiin was full of jokes tonight. Simply offering him the middle finger Emory made her way outgo the bedroom and over to the bathroom to start her shower.

Midway through the shower, she heard the bathroom door open," Lyberti what's wrong?" Emory said.

"I ain't no damn Lyberti," Lessiin said sitting down on the toilet seat waiting.

"Well, what you want?" Emory asked sticking her head out the side of the shower curtain.

"Nothing, I was just making sure you were straight after that *Lessiin* you just got." His jokes continued, and Emory rolled her eyes splashing a little water his way.

"This shit is weird, to me, though," Lessiin said getting back serious.

"What's that?" Emory asked lathering her body up again with soap, she had fallen in love with the custom three sixty shower head in the master bathroom.

"All of this, the kid, the woman, us. All this shit came out of nowhere, but I'm ok with that. Like I knew shit was real when all I could think about was Lyberti, you and flooding these streets but in that order." Lessiin said in a tone that he was confused

"Is that a problem? Is my presence too much for you?" Emory asked turning the shower off and stepping out. Lessiin handed her the towel he had on his lap and shook his head no.

"That's what I'm saying like I don't ever want to be away from you. Yo Em, if you on some fuck shit let me know now ma. I promise you if we get any deeper than we are now, and you play me, I will make a garden on top of yo ass in that backyard." Lessiin said to her staring into her eyes not even blinking.

"Lessiin, you have nothing to worry about baby." Emory kept it short if she hadn't learned anything in short amount of time of being around Lessiin she had learned that actions spoke way louder to him than any words.

"Aight. Now come tuck a nigga in like you do Lyberti, we gotta be up dumb early." Lessiin said wrapping his arms around her waist and guiding her back into the bedroom.

"Who is we? I don't need to be at the meeting in the morning," Emory said thinking she and Lyberti were going to kick back and chill until he was done.

"Like hell, you don't," was all Lessiin said as they walked into the bedroom to find Lyberti knocked out in the center of it.

"This lil nigga gotta go," Lessiin complained.

"Leave him alone, come on big baby. I got both of y'all spoiled." Emory joked walking over to the dresser to grab a t-shirt to sleep in. Once she had thrown it on, she crawled into the bed with both guys, and they fell asleep. For the first time in a long time Emory was at peace if only for those few hours, it was peace.

Landon

"Is there anything else I can get for you Landon?" Jersey asked as she finished filling out his charts with his information she had gathered.

"Naw, I'm straight. But you can send Nurse Ellis back in here for my bath, a nigga feeling dirty." Landon said with a sneaky smirk

"You tried it. Nurse Ellis is off today; I can send Nurse Johnson in here." Jersey joked back waiting on the response from Landon.

"Yo fuck that, Nurse Johnson is a whole dude. Fuck I look like letting that she-man wash me up. I'm gone be a dirty ass patient until y'all have to hose me down in this bitch." Landon fussed remembering how he woke up to 'it' checking his vitals and wished he was still in a coma.

Jersey was bent over laughing because she remembered the exact same thing, she was told by her charge nurse that Landon was acting a damn fool and requested that only she and Nurse Johnson be the 'only muthafuckas' he woke up to.

"You gone get put out if you keep acting a fool," Jersey told him.

"At this point sis, I'm trying to get put out this bitch. Y'all wrong as hell got TiTi up here knowing muthafuckas is waking up from the afterlife and damn sure don't want to look at its ugly ass at first sight." Landon continued to fuss as Jersey roamed around his room making sure everything was good before she started her rounds.

"I'll see you in an hour. Are you sure you don't want that bath now?" Jersey teased.

"Yo, I'm telling Loyal to dump you." Landon joked

"Boy please, your brother loves my dirty drawers. Anyway, I'll send Nurse White in here with your pain meds in about fifteen minutes. You know how to reach me." Jersey said walking out of his door.

Landon was so happy to have a nurse that he somewhat knew. It kept his blood pressure down knowing he didn't have to fight to stay awake thinking one of these nurses was sent to finish him off.

Turning the channel to ESPN, Landon heard his FaceTime going off, so he reached with his unbroken arm to get it. Seeing it was his sister, he hurriedly swiped to connect the call.

"What up Fat Ma?" Landon said smiling.

"You ugly. What you doing?" Leylan said, happier that her brother was awake and responsive.

"Trying to chill but these fucking nurses, well besides Jersey, keep fucking with me. Aye you know them videos we be watching on Facebook with ol boy with the green hair, TiTi? Yeah, that nigga is a nurse up here, I swear." Landon said with a serious face, all you could hear was Leylan cracking up and telling him he was stupid.

"I'm gone come see!" Leylan said egging him on.

"Don't get to asking for no autograph either with your groupie ass" Landon joked.

"Boy, fuck you," Leylan said choking on the weed she had just inhaled.

"Ooh bring ya boy some," Landon said lifting his eyebrows up and down

"It's a no for me dog." Leylan impersonated the American Idol judge Randy Jackson.

"Niggas ain't loyal. But anyway, you about to go to the meeting?"

"Yeah, I'm just waiting on Jream to find his shoes, so we can go," Leylan said loudly so he could hear her.

"Watch out, the boy gotta be fresh." Landon joked, he honestly liked Jream and his sister together.

"Yeah for who? Anyway, I'm gone put you on when we get there, so you don't miss nothing ok?" Leylan said assuring him.

"That's a bet Fat Ma. Let me tell these hoes not to give me these meds yet, so I can focus."

"Okay love you, I'll call in a minute" Leylan disconnected the call just as a knock came at Landon's door. When he told whoever was there to come in, he wished he hadn't.

"Well looks like your recovering quite well Mr. Miahgo." The condescending tone cracked through the small room. Suddenly Landon erupted in a fit of coughs and started wheezing making the detective look around for help.

"Are you okay? Do you need the nurse?" He asked concerned.

"Ye-yeah I'm alright, just allergic to pork that's all," Landon said rolling his eyes and laying back on the bed.

"Quite the jokester, I see." The detective replied sarcastically.

"Mario Finelley," Landon said before turning the volume up on the tv that was mounted to the wall.

"Huh?" The detective was confused at this point.

"I said Mario Finelley, that's my lawyer's name and any questions or concerns you may have or need to be addressed, contact him. Now if you will excuse me, get out, that would greatly appreciate it." Landon said in a cool demeanor.

The detective knew prior to coming up here his task wouldn't be easy, but he thought that maybe if he caught Landon alone that it would be a little easier, but clearly, he was dead wrong.

"One day you're going to need us and then what? I'm just trying to do my protecting and serving." He tried a different angle this time

clap clap clap

"You want a tissue or something? Beat it, sir, Mario Finelley will be more than willing to assist you in protecting and serving," Landon spat becoming agitated. The detective stood at the foot of his bed for about two long minutes before leaving without saying a word.

When Landon was about to push the button for the nurse to bring his meds his phone went off indicating it was a facetime call, again.

Answering and waiting for the call to connect, Landon saw his whole family seated in normal fashion, plus Lyberti ad Loyal.

"Yo!" Landon yelled bringing some smiles around the room.

"Aye Loyal, break up with your girl my nigga. She tried to let a he-bitch give me a bath bro." Landon snitched causing everyone to laugh at his silliness.

"Good to see you're in a good mood G." Loyal responded after the laughter subsided.

"I was. Aye, Where PopPop at? The pigs in blue just left from up here. Sen can you tell Finelley to handle that for ya favorite boy please?" Landon spoke.

"Yes, Fave. Now as far as Cesare, that's why we are all here. Before I get into that, Loyal needs to spill whatever he has, and maybe our puzzle will start coming together more." Seneca spoke sitting at the head of the table. Usually, that spot was claimed by PopPop but obviously it was some shit going on.

Leylan's phone was positioned perfectly so that Landon could see any and everybody in the room. Loyal sat up and placed two black folders on the table, opening one he pulled out one piece of paper and looked around the room at everyone.

"Well I'm Loyal as y'all already know, I grew up out in Raymore with Dimengo's mother, my Big Mama. I only saw him and Laila on occasion for a few hours at a time throughout my life. I'm just a regular ass nigga though, I went to school for computer technology, and I can do just about anything down to stealing your whole existence. I stay out the way though, I volunteer at the community center with the boys and keep them little niggas out of trouble."

"Nigga you sound like trouble, the fuck." Landon interrupted jokingly. Loyal smiled and kept going.

"So, imagine my surprise when my Big Mama calls me up telling me that my 'father' really needs to meet with me. At first, I'm like fuck dude, but Big Mama would have kicked a nigga ass. Long story short though, I met up with dude and he tells me about the triplets and how he needed my help taking everything they had." Loyal had maintained eye contact with everyone in the room during his story, and that was giving off nothing short of good vibes

"I tell him straight up; I'm not a killer cause I'm not. He goes on to tell me that he needs me to tap into every single personal file on the Miahgo name. I'm thinking cool, but how is the information I provide going to help with the type of time you on. So, I play along, I go in and find out some general records type shit, so I can find y'all."

"What made you want to go against dude? I mean not that you made the wrong decision, but why?" Leylan interrupted wanting to know.

"I live by my name." Loyal stated keeping its short and simple. Lessiin sat back in the rolling chair observing everything. He liked everything about his little brother, he wasn't out here trying to be something he wasn't and he damn sure wasn't trying to come up off his name, which he could. That earned him nothing but respect from Lessiin which was major.

"While I was finding out how to find y'all, I also ran across some ill shit. Yo Landon do you know Essynce Powell?" Loyal asked causing Leylan and Lessiin to stare directly in his direction on the phone.

Landon's eyebrow's furrowed at the question before answering, "Yeah, she was in the car with me at the races when Chewbacca tried to take us out. But her last name ain't Powell, it's Reid."

"Yeah, that's her jacket name. Essynce is a Federal Agent. Special Agent Powell. Yo Lessiin have you heard of Special Agent Miles?" You could hear a rat piss on cotton is was deathly quiet in the room. As if Emory could read minds she stood up grabbing Lyberti's hand and rushed out of the room taking him to another office and turning on a movie on her phone to keep him occupied.

Returning back into the room, Emory noticed everyone still in their same positions only all eyes were tuned in on Lessiin. His eyes were closed, and his body was still. If it wasn't for the rise and fall of his chest, they would have been checking his pulse.

"Are you telling me both of them are Federal Agents?" Seneca asked in disgust.

"I knew it was some shit with those bitches when I saw them together!" Leylan screamed slamming her hand on the table. "I saw them at the cheesecake factory together that day before she popped up at Lessiin's crib," Leylan said in a whisper internally kicking her own ass for not digging into it.

"You didn't think that shit was suspect?" Lessiin asked coldly.

"Hold up, not like that you won't! The bitches told me they were long lost cousins and I never viewed Nefe as the pig type, a ghetto ass rat bitch but not a fucking Fed!"

"Landon when I told you that bitch's eyes weren't right, what did you tell me?" Lessiin continued still not opening his eyes.

"Lessiin you can miss with that shit my nigga!" Landon yelled before disconnecting the call. Deep down Landon knew his brother was right all along, but the fact of the matter was that he just didn't get that vibe from Essynce.

Normally he would have run a background check on anybody he would be potentially bringing around his family. For some reason he didn't feel the need to do so with Essynce, she was so sexually awkward and at times shy and corky, he would have been just as shocked as he was now had he learned she was a Fed. Landon's body was on fire, and just as he was about to push the button for the nurse, Jersey came rushing into the room.

"What's the matter? Your heart rate is through the roof!" Jersey exclaimed pulling out her stethoscope and reading the monitors around.

"How long I got to stay in here?" Landon asked in a cold demeanor.

"It'll be a minute Landon. What has you so upset, you were just fine thirty minutes ago." Jersey logged his pulse and stepped back to look at him.

"I'm straight. Look I need you to ask that doctor what's up? I need to go, I'll walk up out this bitch with this little dress shit on if I have to." Landon declared.

"Ok keep calm alright. I don't need you walking around with your ass out. I'll go have a talk with your doctor and see what's what ok?" Jersey turned to leave out, but stopped when Landon called out to her.

"Can you see if there's an Essynce Powell up here?" Landon's blood was boiling, and he needed answers like yesterday.

"I can't tell you that," Jersey said with a questioning stare.

"I don't want to know her blood type fam, I just want to know if she is currently in this hospital. She was in the car when I wrecked, and I just want to make sure she ain't in the morgue." Landon manipulated

"I'll see what I can do," Jersey said before continuing her stride out the door. The wheels in Landon's head were spinning.

Jream

"Lessiin what the fuck?!" Leylan screamed out jumping up from her chair.

"Calm down Leylan, let Loyal finish first," Jream said wrapping his arms around Leylan. Her chest was heaving up and down, her body was hot, so he knew she was about to explode. After about two minutes of Leylan staring menacingly at her brother, she sat down slowly. Jream returned to his seat and listened while Loyal started back telling the information he had.

"As I was saying, Agent Powell and Agent Miles are both Federal agents with one assignment, infiltrate the Miahgo Clan and take them down. Agent Miles has been trying to get Laila and Dimengo to help them in their efforts but to no avail. That's where your grandfather comes into play. He has gone 'off the grid' so that he can take care of your problems."

"Why wouldn't he let us help him?" Leylan interrupted getting more upset by the minute.

"Your grandfather is a very very intelligent man, if he feels that he can control this situation, then he is," Rocky spoke for the first time in the meeting. It was him who found out where Cesare was and why, so he understood the need for the triplets to fall back and let him handle things until needed.

"Anything else?" Lessiin said coldly looking at Loyal.

"Nah," Loyal said shortly sitting back in his chair looking around the room.

"Okay, my turn. So, with the information that we now know, we are going to have to reach out to some old friends and find out just how much shit the Feds have at this point. Leylan, I need you to get with Taylen and find out where they are hiding Essynce. Now I know why they wouldn't let us see her when the wreck happened. Lessiin I need you to get with Malia and get this case under control." Seneca said standing up and taking over the role that Cesare normally would.

"Oh, one more thing, we need to know exactly who that body belonged too that was in that trunk." She added

"I can help with that. Do y'all know a Tarenzo Lindsey?" Loyal asked already having got into the records at the local police station.

"Renzo?!" Everyone said at the same time except Emory and Jream.

"That's the person who they identified in the trunk." Loyal stated in a matter of fact tone.

"This shit getting weird. How the fuck Renzo end up dead and in my fucking trunk?" Lessiin exclaimed.

"I'm about to call Thiago," Rocky said while dismissing himself.

"I got some shit to do, Leylan don't make me come hunt your ass down ma. Meet me at my crib by nine." Jream warned giving Leylan a kiss on the check before saying his departing words to everyone else.

Lessiin stood up without saying a word and left out the room, getting closer to the door where Lyberti was he heard the sounds of the game he must have been playing and walked in the room closing it behind him. Lyberti glanced up for a quick second to acknowledge him and turned his attention back to the phone.

Lessiin stood there just staring at his son as he watched him touch and maneuver the screen. Lessiin was in a terrible head space and just being around Lyberti was keeping him from snapping. For about ten minutes Lessiin just sat there and stared at Lyberti as he contently played on the phone.

"Pops, I got to pee" Lyberti said looking at his father. Lessiin nodded his head standing up as they both walked out the room towards the bathroom. Lessiin opened the bathroom door and turned the light on for him and left out. While Lessiin leaned against the wall in a zone thinking he felt the comfort he needed. Emory wrapped her arms around Lessiin and held him. She didn't say anything and neither did he, but her presence relaxed him.

Lyberti came out the bathroom a minute later and looked at them. He walked over to the two of them and tried to wrap his little arms around them. The site was definitely a Kodak moment as the small 'family' bonded. Lessiin pulled away from them and spoke.

"Come on lil nigga, it's time to go." Lessiin said while grabbing Emory's hand.

"Going home?" Lyberti asked running past him and to the door

"Yeah." Lessiin said amused at how upbeat Lyberti always seemed to be.

The three of them walked outside towards Emory's car. Lessiin saw a head already in there and on instinct he pulled out his heat.

"Relax, it's your sister." Emory said while rolling her eyes.

"The fuck she riding with us for?" Lessiin said loud enough for her to hear. Leylan stuck her middle out the window, causing Lessiin to chuckle.

Once everybody was in the car, and Lyberti started talking everyone's ears off, the ride was otherwise quiet. Pulling up to Lessiin's town home, Emory and Lyberti got out. Once saying their goodbyes Lessiin pulled off after they made it in the house.

Leylan ruffled around in her purse eventually pulling out an already rolled blunt that she hurriedly sparked and mellowed her nerves. Passing the blunt to her brother the two never said a word as they enjoyed their session passing the blunt back and forth. Pulling up to the hospital, Lessiin tossed the roach and hopped out the car heading straight for his brother's room.

"You come in here talking that shit and I swear to God I'll shoot the fuck out you right in your boney ass arm," Landon fired off as soon as his door opened, and he saw it was his siblings.

"Shoot me with what nigga?" Lessiin teased.

"Anyway, you left the meeting having a temper tantrum and shit, so we came to tell you what's up cry baby." Leylan said sitting on the end of the bed.

"You shut your chunky ass up girl. This Snoop Dogg reject looking muthafucka over there had me fucked up. Wasnt nobody crying bout shit, for one. For two, I don't want to hear shit unless y'all coming to break a nigga out this bitch." Landon said.

"Break you out of here, why?" Leylan asked.

"Cause the bitch ass doctor talking bout I have to stay here another week and I'm not! I'm ready to go," Landon said getting frustrated thinking about the conversation he just had with the doctor.

"We'll see about that, but look, that body that was in my whip was Renzo." Lessiin started but stopped when he heard the door to the room come open. On instinct the triplets grabbed their guns ready for whatever only to see it was Loyal.

"Why you got a gun under your pillow fool?" Leylan laughed sitting back down on the bed.

"Shit mother dearest around this bitch trying to take a nigga out, I got to be on my toes at all times. Plus, the pain pills be having a nigga out of it, so I'm gone shoot first and ask never." Landon shrugged his one shoulder.

"Like I was saying, Rocky went to go get Thiago on the line and find out some shit. I'm trying to figure out who was tough enough to get that close to Renzo. They did that nigga dirty and then left his ass in my whip. Shit don't even make sense." Lessiin said.

"I'm gone tell you what I think and then we can go paint the streets.I think that boy Feliz had something to do with it. Ain't it a coincidence that Renzo reaches out to us murk him and then all of a sudden, we got the feds on our ass and Dimengo and Laila on some good bullshit. I think Feliz had Renzo murked and put in your whip and framed you trying to knock out two birds with one stone." Leylan said.

"Yeah that's saying a little bit, but if they had Essynce and Nefe working with the Feds then why would that little body be of importance?" Lessiin asked.

"Yo, where is PopPop?" Landon asked.

"Oh, he went off the grid to get control of shit." Leylan said smartly using her fingers to make air quotes.

"I need to get a track on that fucking Dimengo." Lessiin said.

"I got a meeting with Dimengo in two hours. Why don't y'all rock and hear what you can?" Loyal suggested.

"Where?" The triplets said at the same time.

"Yo do y'all do that corny shit all the time?" Loyal joked.

"Just them two, mostly." Lessiin chuckled pointing at Leylan and Landon who laughed nodding their heads in agreeance.

"We are meeting at Gates on 47th at 12:30." Loyal said as someone knocked at the door.

"Got damn my room stay jumping. Come in!" Landon said rolling his eyes slightly.

"Mr. Miahgo are you ready for your bath now?" Nurse Johnson asked as she wheeled cart in. The freak in Landon got excited as he shook his head yes motioning for all his siblings to get out. They laughed filing out the room. Lessiin and Leylan knew they needed to get prepared for the meeting Loyal had with Dimengo.

Nefe

Walking into the small restaurant Nefe looked around unit she spotted Dimengo. Walking over to the table she sat down while he eyed her lustfully. Just as she was about to say something she saw Laila coming over to the table. She looked at Laila as she walked confidently through the restaurant. If you didn't know them personally, you would never guess they were some coke heads.

Laila came to the table and offered a small smile before pulling her chair up to the table. Dimengo's lustful gaze still hadn't changed even with the presence of Laila now at the table. Nefe shook her head and cleared her throat before speaking.

"So, what's up? Why did we need to meet suddenly?" she asked opting to just give Laila eye contact for now.

"What's up with this plan man? Now I did my part, I got rid of that nigga Renzo and made it look like it was on Lessiin. I had Laila go up there to the hospital to take care of Landon. This shit needs to kick up a notch." Dimengo demanded

"First of all, she didn't even finish the job. Second, we all know Lessiin isn't going down for that body considering the footage won't show him outside of his brother's room prior to the time he got caught." Nefe had to get Dimengo together occasionally because he thought he could talk crazy to anybody.

"Well what the fuck you wanted me to do hold on to the fucking body until he came out?" Dimengo whispered harshly.

"He left a note on our car," Laila blurted out.

"What note? And who is he?" Nefe said apparently over this little shindig.

"Lessiin. He said we would be receiving a Lessiin in death soon. Or some shit like that," Laila said starting feel the effects of the cocaine wearing off. She was getting antsy.

"That's it? Chile, you are tripping, why would Lessiin be leaving y'all a note he has no idea about y'all or your involvement yet." Nefe chumped her off

"Your fucking son told them!" Laila said getting loud causing people to look over in their direction.

"Keep your fucking voice down. Now tell me what you are talking about Lyberti told them what?" Nefe said between clenched teeth.

"When Landon flatlined, we were all rushed into the family room. When Lyberti saw me, he yelled out granny. Leylan asked his little smart ass how he knew who I was, and he said that I go eat with his mama all the time." Laila said sounding annoyed more than anything.

"Why the fuck would you go up there trying to kill him anyway?!" Nefe said now raising her voice.

"Aye aye aye, listen fuck all that. What's up Nefe? How much longer before y'all take these muthafuckas down. Shit we been helping you for the longest and I don't see shit rewarding yet." Dimengo jumped in trying to get to the point of the meeting.

"Oh, trust you have been rewarded. Anyway, let me think on this shit, and we will meet back here Sunday. Try not to do no more dumb shit." Nefe spat before getting up from the table and sauntering out the restaurant.

"I don't trust that bitch." Laila said lowly and if she knew the truth she really would hate Nefe. Dimengo shook his head thinking the same thing.

"Come on, Loyal got some shit that will have us set for a minute." Dimengo ordered as the couple left out the small restaurant headed to another across town.

Essynce

"Can I have my phone?" Essynce asked her mother frustrated. For the past week they had been treating her like an invalid and she was sick of it.

"Did you take your medicine Essynce?" her mother asked completely ignoring her phone request.

"Yes. Now phone please?" Essynce responded annoyed.

"The doctors say you need rest. I don't think your phone will help with that." Mrs. Powell insisted. Fed up with the baby treatment she felt she was receiving, Essynce got up slowly heading towards the front door of her parent's ranch style home.

"Where are you going?" Mrs. Powell asked.

"Out of here! I don't care if I have to hitchhike, I won't stand for this. I'm not a child," Essynce said.

"Calm down, I'm just trying to help my child," she said getting up heading to the kitchen to retrieve Essynce's cell phone. "Here you go, now go have a seat and I'll fix lunch shortly," Mrs. Powell said rolling her eyes and walking away from her daughter.

Essynce slowly sat back down and powered her phone on. Once it finally came up she was surprised to see all the get well wishes she was receiving from her colleagues. Ignoring them she scrolled her phone looking for the person she needed.

"Hello."

"Nefe, it's Essynce."

"What's up?'

"What's going on, I've been off the grid since I didn't transfer to that other hospital. Catch me up," Essynce asked eagerly. She really wanted to ask about Landon, but decided on a different angle.

"Why didn't you go to the hospital Essynce?' Nefe asked.

"I can't rest in that place, I'm at my parents." Essynce said quickly.

"Well nothing, everything is under control. Just get some rest," Nefe said trying to rush her off the phone.

"Nefe don't lie to me!" Essynce slightly elevated her voice. She was fed up with everyone treating her like she was fragile glass.

"Hello? Nefe you there?" Essynce looked at her phone to see her home screen display indicating that Nefe had hung up on her. Deciding she wasn't done she called her captain.

"This is Alexander."

"Cap, this is Essynce."

"Essynce? Where are you? Why aren't you in the new location?" He fired off.

"I'm at my parents' house. I'm ready to report back. I've been resting for about a week and just need to be briefed on what I need to be doing at this point regarding the case." Essynce said with authority.

"There's nothing that needs to be done right now. As far as the case is concerned, it's being handled." Alexander stated shutting down any thoughts Essynce had.

"Thank you, sir." Essynce replied defeated, hanging up before he could say anything more. Deciding to make one last call, she held her breath as her hands became clammy and her rate sped up. On the fourth ring she was going to hang up, but then it picked up, and the voice she hadn't heard in so long came through. In a chilling tone the two words he spoke felt like daggers being shot through her chest.

"Your dead." Landon spat holding the phone observing her background.

"I know you heard me." Was the last thing he said before disconnecting the call. Essynce shaking hands dropped her phone making a loud thud on the hardwood floors. Mrs. Powell came rushing in the living room alarmed by the noise.

"Are you alright? Essynce what's wrong, why are you crying baby?" Mrs. Alexander asked concerned.

"I-I'm fine. Just frustrated front this leg pain. My meds haven kicked in yet," Essynce lied with ease. What she really wanted to do was break down in a fit. She was scared and couldn't tell her mother a thing.

"Well have a seat, I made some sandwiches, I'll bring you one and then you can lay down and let the meds do their job." Mrs. Alexander said.

"Ok" Essynce said just above a whisper.

As she bent down slowly to pick up her phone she had an idea. She had to go to therapy tomorrow and when she did she was going to get away from her mother. She texted her only friend and asked her if she could pick her up after her session and she said yes. Essynce's plan was forming slowly.

Loyal

Sitting in the back of the semi crowded Gates BBQ spot Loyal waited to see Dimengo's slimy ass slither in the doors. From where he was sitting he could see the door clearly and there was only one way in and out of the spot, so he knew he would be the first person Dimengo saw when he walked in.

Late just like he suspected he would be Dimengo strolled in looking like he was that nigga, but Loyal knew the deal. He watched as Laila strutted in behind him and hated the ground his so-called parents walked on. Loyal didn't feel like he missed out on shit by not having his absentee parents, but after working with the teens at the center, he often saw the adverse effect parentless homes had on kids.

His Big Mama did a damn good job at raising the man before them, but it wasn't her job. Big Mama didn't lay down and have Loyal, Dimengo and Laila did. In fact, they had four children and failed miserably at raising any of them. The fact that Dimengo really felt like the triplets owed him even a salt grain of respect baffled Loyal.

As the two made their way over to the table, Loyal heard Lessiin tell him that he got visual of the pair. Loyal had set up his own wire type device so that Lessiin and Leylan could have a clear audio of the meeting. They didn't plan on confronting the duo today, but they at least wanted to follow them once they left so that they could get the one up on them when the time presented itself.

"Hello Loyal." Laila said leaning forward to hug him, but Loyal stuck his hand out for a handshake instead. Laila looked at his hand as if it had shit on it.

"Really?" she huffed leaving his hand out and taking a seat next to Dimengo with a sour look on her face. Loyal chuckled unfazed by her sour demeanor, what more did she expect.

"Alright, so I asked you here, so you could let me know what's up on that info I asked you for." Dimengo said taking a swig of his water the waitress had brought to the table.

"Oh, I'm fine, you know shit like that. How you doing?" Loyal responded sarcastically, not that he really cared how Dimengo was doing, but it was the principle of the matter. Loyal liked playing games with Dimengo anyway.

"Anyway, what's up?" Dimengo said getting frustrated.

"Laila do you ever talk without being told to?" Loyal poked adding fuel to Dimengo's fire.

"Lil nigga quit stalling, if you don't have the shit, just say it. Shit you want my attention or something? I know we wasn't shit and quite frankly you don't look like you are hurting for shit bruh. So, if you trying to bond or some shit, you are barking up the wrong tree." Dimengo said causing Loyal to lean forward laughing at the end of his speech.

"You think I want or need something from you muthafuckas? Do you? You got me fucked up *pops*, my nigga you came looking for me. I didn't send for you. Don't take these smart-ass remarks for anything more than that homie. I never once cried for you or her, if anything I pitied my Big Mama for always having faith in her fucked-up ass son." Glass shattered on the floor as Dimengo lunged for Loyal across the table missing the front of his shirt by an inch.

Loyal knew he struck a nerve so as soon as he saw Dimengo bust a move he pushed his chair back quickly.

"Dimengo please." Laila pleaded.

"Dimengo please what? That's your problem, this nigga was about to harm your child and the first thing out your mouth is Dimengo? Y'all muthafuckas deserve each other. Fuck you and her, find out what you need on your own *mom and dad.*" Loyal stood up adjusting the windbreaker jacket he had on and pulling his pants up just in case Dimengo wanted to shoot the fair one. Loyal may not have been a killer, but his hands were lethal and down for whatever. As he walked around Dimengo and a frightened looking Laila he never waived eye contact. Dimengo was huffing and puffing like a raging bull, if looks could kill Loyal would be kissing the dirt by now.

One thing about Dimengo, he knew when to hold and when to fold them. Firing off on Loyal sounded like a great idea but he knew he wouldn't win, so he let his son have that, for now.

"You folks enjoy the rest of your day. Don't call my phone moving forward." Loyal said with a slight smirk at the end before turning his back and leaving out the door of the restaurant.

Laila released the breath she didn't know she was holding but didn't say a word, she didn't move either. She knew Dimengo quite well so at this point anything was sure to set him off and she wasn't trying to be at the end of his rage right now if she didn't have to be.

When Loyal made it out he slightly jogged over to his awaiting Monte Carlo before jumping in and starting the engine. He waited about ten minutes and watched as Dimengo and Laila walked out of the BBQ restaurant and headed to their car. Loyal already knew that Leylan had placed the tracking device on it so there was no need to follow them, from here on out they would know their every move.

Seeing Lessiin pull out in traffic, Loyal followed suit passing Dimengo and Laila honking his horn. He had to fuck with Dimengo one last time for the day and seeing him throw the middle finger up at him in his rearview let Loyal know his job was well done. Chuckling at his own childish antics, Loyal turned his song up and bobbed his head following his brother and sister in traffic.

Malia

"Please don't tell me the state doesn't have enough evidence to nail these bastards!" Feliz yelled, growing frustrated with the young beautiful prosecutor.

"Mr. Alexander, language! As I was saying, the state now has to take into consideration the footage that has been provided by the hospital." Malia explained as she could see the steam radiating from Alexander's head.

"But they said the cameras in the garage didn't work!" He yelled.

"Correct, but the cameras inside the hospital in the lobby and the floor that Mr. Miahgo was visiting show him entering on Monday and not leaving the floor for any reason aside from the day and time of the incident in question." Malia said sternly, she was getting fed up with the chief of police and the FBI. They wanted the Miahgo's so bad, but they forever failed to dot their I's and cross their T's.

"So how the fuck did the body get there?" Feliz asked.

"Mr. Alexander this will be my last and final warning regarding your language in my office. Now as far as the body in the trunk, I believe that is your job to figure out and bring me the evidence of such. Gentlemen, we have been here time and time again, if you all are so passionate about this family you all are going to have to bring me solid concrete facts and nothing short thereof." Malia stood up from her chair and held her hand out gesturing for the door.

"I swear to God, every time we present something to you about this family you find a way to discredit every piece." Lieutenant Alexander stated still sitting in the chair.

"Well, I'm sorry you feel that way Lieutenant. However, my job is to represent the state of Missouri effectively, I can not do that with half ass evidence that wouldn't hold up in court. Now if that is all, you two gentlemen may see yourselves out." Malia stated coldly standing confidently on what she said.

"What about the weed?" Feliz asked.

"Now we both know that little amount of weed will barely get both individuals a slap on the wrist, we are talking a fine and S.I.S probation at the max. If what you all are so desperate for is for this family to go down for whatever you all think you know I need stone cold hard evidence, a witness willing to testify or a confession, that simple." Malia stated feeling like a broken record at this point.

Getting up the twins walked towards the door and opened it exiting the office without another word. Once she was sure they were at least on the elevator Malia let out a huge breath, this case was stressing her out. The loyalty she had dedicated to the Miahgo's was strong. Sure, indeed she had received the footage from the parking garage and she viewed it, what she saw had her questioning so many things. When she got in contact with Cesare and handed over the footage to him, he promised her like he did all those years ago that he had it all under control, and she believed him.

Taking a seat, she turned her chair towards the window that held an amazing view of the city's skyline. Whenever she was having a rough day and thinking about giving everything up she would just sit and gaze out of the window until she felt better.

"You still daydreaming I see." The baritone voice came through the room causing her to jump in fear.

"Don't you knock?" Malia said once she caught her breath.

"Have I ever?" He said back as he shuffled some papers on her desk making room to sit.

"Still rude as fuck," Malia griped

"Ohh potty mouth Miss State Prosecutor." He teased her.

"How can I help you Lessiin?" Malia asked trying to avoid his stare. After all this time Malia still got butterflies whenever she was in Lessiin's presence. She had no idea why he had that type of control over her mental, but he did.

"From what I hear, you are doing your thing. I just came to check on my fam, aint like we run in the same circles and shit. Nigga gotta be in trouble with the laws to see your face. Or shit the holidays." Lessiin said sarcastically.

"Sounds like you miss me or something Lessiin, let me find out. Is your new little stripper girl not doing her job?" Malia asked with jealousy dripping from her pores.

"Jealousy isn't a good color on you kid." Lessiin said touching her chin. See Lessiin knew Malia had always had a crush on him from the time they found her in that field and brought her back. For years she would do anything she could to get Lessiin to notice her and he did, but he never once acted on it. Lessiin didn't see Malia in that way and never would, but he still used every opportunity he could to fuck with her.

"You wish. But what's up, why are you here? You just missed your two biggest cheerleaders." Malia said trying to busy herself by moving papers around. She was really trying to keep from gazing at Lessiin.

"I saw them fags, but they didn't see me. I been here peeping out the scene and shit, you know. But I'm here because if nobody else knows, you do. Where is Cesare?" Lessiin asked her without a hint laughter as before

"Lessiin don't..." Malia started but Lessiin put his hand up to stop her

"Don't bullshit me Malia Rose. Where. Is. Cesare.?" Lessiin said slowly.

"I can't tell you that because he asked me not to. But I can tell you that he will be getting in contact with you soon. Lessiin please don't start that lurking shit that you do, he said he will get with you when the time is right." Malia said sounding like that teenage girl Lessiin remembered.

"Lurking? You got me fucked up." Lessiin said laughing knowing she was telling the truth. One of Lessiin's strengths was stalking his prey, he was a beast for real and his whole family knew it.

"You're laughing because you know exactly what I mean. Anyway, you're good as far as your case goes. Tell Jream he needs to come see me, I need to know some things I couldn't find."

"I aint no damn secretary, tell that nigga Finelley to tell him." Lessiin said getting up to leave the office.

"You're an asshole." Malia said shaking her head.

"Thank you." Lessiin said without turning around and exiting her office unnoticed the same way he came. Malia looked at the clock and saw that it was going on 4:30 and she was calling it a day. She had a date at seven anyway and needed to go home and figure out what she was wearing. As she closed her computer down and gathered her things, she left out of her office and hopped on the elevator to get to the parking garage.

Making it to her car she waited for her phone to connect to her Bluetooth before heading to her condo that was about five blocks from her office. Speaking to the doorman she made her way upstairs and kicked off the heels that weren't made for walking. Malia wasn't your typical looking State Prosecutor, she was the youngest graduate in her law class and she would be damned if she looked anything like those stuffy ass colleagues of hers. Every suit she had was tailored to fit her curvy frame, leaving her looking sexy, yet very conservative edgy. Having a standing appointment every Wednesday with the Dominican shop she frequented her naturally curly hair stayed slayed for the Gawds!!

Walking around in her bra and panties, Malia made her way to her walk in closet trying to figure out what she was going to wear for this date. This was the second time her and Dez had been out together and he seemed like a nice guy.

Finally deciding on black one-piece jumpsuit with slits down the front, she paired it with an olive-green blazer and matching olive green high-top Air Force Ones. Going for a sexy casual look considering they were just going to Top Golf. Texting Dez to find out if he was picking her up or were they meeting each other there, Malia decided to hop in the shower while she waited for him to text back.

Enjoying her shower for a good twenty-five minutes, Dez had text back that he would be downstairs to pick her up around seven fifteen. Moisturizing her body while looking at the clock Malia saw she had plenty of time to waste so she decided to call her sister and kill some time.

"Whose ass I need to beat?" she answered on the third ring

"Why are you so violent? And keep calm there's no asses that need beating." Malia laughed

"I'm just saying, you don't call anymore so I thought it was an issue that needed to be pressed. What you doing?" she asked.

"Just got off and out the shower, I got a little date later so I'm killing time. What you got going?"

"Aw so you bored and decided to call my ass huh? Girl bye! I aint chopped liver!"

"Leylan why are you so dramatic?" Malia asked laughing.

"Shit, you know me. But anyway, what's tea on the date? Who is he? Where did y'all meet? What's his social?" Leylan said in one breath.

"Whoa whoa whoa! Wait now, first his name is Dez. I met him at the gym. This is only the second date. And no ma'am you are not getting his social so that you can run a background check." Malia answered already knowing what was up.

"It's too much going on right now for new people Malia Rose! I need to know who, what, when, where, why and how." Leylan stressed. Being the youngest and only girl of the triplets had left Leylan with little to know authority growing up. So, when Malia came along, the girls bonded and Leylan took on the role as the big sister and she wore it like a badge of honor.

"Chill Leylan alright. It ain't even like that, he aint even from the town so there's nothing to worry about." Malia said trying to convince her.

"That's all the more reason for you to let me run his social Malia." Leylan pushed.

"You need to be running this." Jream could be heard in the background and Malia could only imagine what was going on over there considering Leylan started giggling.

"Malia text me where y'all are going at least and one in between and when you get home. Oh, and his license plate number." Leylan ran down.

"Goodbye!" Malia laughed trying to rush her off the phone, she could hear Leylan yell she was for real before she disconnected the call. Shaking her head, she really did miss the Miahgo's. She couldn't really hang with them out in the open do to their line of work and her profession so any time they all got together it was in private settings. Nobody knew of their connection and that's how they planned to keep it.

Seeing that it was now 5:45 she got up to finish getting ready. Deciding she wanted to beat her face since she couldn't during the week, she laid all her makeup out on the bathroom counter and got to work. About twenty minutes later she was pleased and taking pictures sending them to Leylan to show her skills.

After putting her clothes on and setting her curly mane with a deep side part, Malia was ready to go. She had about twenty more minutes before Dez said he would be there, so she took her time switching her purses to match her outfit. Right on time her phone went off and instead of answering Dez, she locked her door and met him down in the lobby.

"I thought you fell asleep on a nigga." Dez said looking at her like she was a full course meal.

"Nope I didn't. You like what you see or you what?" Malia asked laughing at his stuck expression.

"Like? I love that shit ma, you look different every time I see you." Dez said walking up to her with his arms out for a hug.

"Now that you mention it, I probably do." Malia laughed thinking about the few other times they had seen each other, and she definitely had a different look each time. She was diverse like that though. She could stand up against anyone in the courtroom and turn around and throw her Jordan's on and look like an around the way girl with no problem.

"That's sexy. You ready?" Dez asked placing his hand in the small of her back guiding her out the door of the condos.

"These are nice little spots down here, I need to check them out." Dez admired.

"Where do you stay and how long will you be here?" Malia asked as she slid in the seat of the charcoal grey charger. Closing the door, Dez swaggered around to the driver's side before sliding in and adjusting the heat and music.

"I stay out south, ain't that what y'all call it? Out there off 95th, but I'll be here til my business is taken care of ma." Dez said following the instructions of the GPS to get them to their destination.

"Oh ok, so we didn't really to get to do too much talking last time in the movies. Tell me a little about yourself," Malia said as she turned her body towards him to give him her undivided attention.

"Nothing much to tell. You already know, I'm from St. Louis, I'm down here to take care of some business, I'm pretty much black and white ma. I'm a chill dude now, I hit a bump in the road of life a little while back and it helped get my head right. What about you?" Dez asked as he whipped in and out of traffic.

"Same, I don't look like what I've been through so that's a blessing. I'm born and raised here, I went to school to be successful and now I am." Malia shrugged.

"You real humble and shit, I can tell." Dez commented.

"Well when you've been through what I've been through you learn to be. In the blink an eye anything can be snatched away from you." Malia said.

"I dig that ma. So, on a lighter note, you any good at golf?" Dez asked wanting to lighten the mood up a little bit.

"Heck no! I'm competitive and I hate losing," Malia laughed but she was dead ass serious.

"Aye low key, I don't know shit about golf ma. I googled 'nice date spots in Kansas City' and this hoe popped up," Dez said causing Malia to burst out laughing at his honesty.

"Well I heard the drinks and food was cool, so we should be good either way." Malia said as she heard the GPS say they were one mile away from their destination.

Dez and Malia had a good time at Top Golf, both not knowing what they were doing, but they enjoyed each other's company. On the ride back to Malia's condo she dozed off and didn't wake up until she felt Dez lightly shaking her.

"We at you crib ma, wake up." Dez said in a low tone. When Malia finally opened her eyes and stared into Dez's, something came over her. So, she acted on it and leaned forward kissing him on his full lips. Malia brought her hand up and placed it on the side of Dez face as their kiss deepened. She felt his strong hand gripping her thigh and pulled back.

"Uhm, do you want to come in?" Malia asked trying to catch her breath

"Listen ma, I'm not that nigga you think I am. I'm not, I repeat not going to come up there and talk all night. I'm just gone be straight up with you. So, if you want to keep our shit in the friend area its best that I don't come up there." Dez said being brutally honest.

"Who said I wanted to keep it in the friendly area?" Malia asked as she got out the charger and headed for the door. Dez turned the car off and followed her inside and up to her condo. When they got inside Dez looked around and liked what he saw. Of course, it was girly as fuck, but he didn't expect anything less. Malia grabbed his hand guiding him towards her bedroom.

"You want a drink?" Malia asked as she took her blazer and shoe off.

"What you got?" Dez asked as he followed suit taking his north face jacket and timberland boots off.

"Hennessey, Cîroc, Wine, Water, Sprite, Coke, Juice" Malia named

"Hennessey no ice ma," Dez answered as he watched her walkout the bedroom and into the kitchen. Shortly after he followed her and watched her as she moved around the kitchen as if she was nervous.

"You good ma? I told you we can keep shit cordial, a nigga ain't pressed," Dez said.

"No! No, it's not that, so listen I'm gone tell you something, but I don't want your pity on nothing like that. Remember how I told you that I went through some shit when I was younger that shaped my life now?" Malia threw a shot of Hennessy back before she continued.

"Well my homegirl and I went to a party and long story short we got kidnapped and gangraped for a week. She died, and I was left for dead and saved. Well I haven't had any type of sex since then, so I say all that to say I'm just nervous about losing my virginity willingly that's all." Malia was definitely feeling the effects of the liquor she had from Top Golf and the two shots she had just thrown back because she was talking fast and animated.

Dez grabbed the drink she made for him and through it back as well before he spoke. "I don't know if you want to experience that with me ma. I ain't that nigga yet. That's something you want to share with a nigga that's not just tryna chill." In true Dez fashion he kept it all the way real with Malia, he walked up to her placing a kiss on her forehead.

"You're a dope ass female baby, a fucking dime. I'm just not that nigga. I can fuck you, shit I can fuck the lining out that pussy, but that ain't the type of shit you deserve. I'm liable to handle my business tomorrow and hit that highway back home without a word." Dez said rubbing her back while he stood close to her looking her in her eyes while he talked.

"I understand" Malia said putting her head down in embarrassment.

"Naw ma, don't do that. Don't ever feel embarrassed bout shit. You go for how you feel and that was how you was feeling. If I was a real grimy nigga I would have had you screaming my government by now. But that ain't this, feel me beautiful?" Dez said to her pulling a smile from her tipsy face.

"Thank you Dez, seriously." Malia stood on her toes and placed a quick kiss on his lips and stepped out of his embrace before she considered telling him to go ahead and bend her over in the middle of the kitchen.

"It's late; you can stay in my second bedroom if you like." Malia offered.

"Nah ma, I'm gone head back out south so the temptation doesn't get too heavy in here. I'm still a man at the end of the day." They both laughed as they walked back to her bedroom so that he could slip his jacket and boots back on.

"Yo Malia, you owe me another date though." Dez told her giving her a hug and turning around to leave. Malia closed the door and shook her head at herself, turning out the lights she went to bed with thoughts of what ifs with Dez swimming through her head.

Jream

"What you mean she ain't told you that? I'm telling you!" Jream yelled at his uncle, frustrated with the conversation.

"What you better do is take some of that fucking base out your voice when you're talking to me." Rome said ready to two piece his only nephew. He understood where he was coming from and he respected it, but still he wasn't going to get buck.

"You got that Unc, but what I said still remains the same." Jream said to him not so hostile.

"Listen, I respect what you're saying as a man. But understand that this is business, Bliss doesn't work for you, she works for me. The day she walks in here and says, 'Rome I quit," I will grant that. You are my bartender, remember that." Rome said returning his attention back to the paperwork he was handling before Jream came in making demands.

"Yeah okay, she'll be here in an hour." Jream stated getting up.

"Let me ask you a question nephew, does Bliss want to stop dancing or do you want her to stop?" Rome asked placing his papers down and leaning back in his chair.

"She never needed to be stripping; you know who she really is now. So, we both know she never needed to dance, she wanted to be on her solo kick. Well, she is my woman and all that bratty independent woman shit is null and void." Jream said with authority and Rome shook his head chuckling.

He had never seen his nephew so adamant about something, he had no choice but to respect it, and he did. He just wanted to talk to Bliss, all this time she had been working for him in his club and he had no idea who she really was. He and Cesare go way back, he would have never allowed his granddaughter to dance in his establishment purely out of respect. It bothered Rome that it was something about Bliss that made him a little more protective of her more than the others. He always felt she had some shit about her that set apart from the other girls, and now he knew why.

"I'm just asking. So, you know the type of family you're getting yourself involved with. Don't look at me like that youngin, I'm just rapping with you on some real shit. I know you have zero bitch in your blood, shit I damn near helped raised your little ass. I'm just asking are you fully aware?" Rome had a serious look on his face talking to his only nephew.

"Yeah Unc, I do." Jream said shortly not feeling like he owed anybody an explanation. If they truly knew him then they knew how he rocked and that was all that needed to be said. Rome shook his head in admiration, Jream was just like his father, Rome's little brother. He had the heart of a lion and nothing or no one walking the face of the earth pumped fear in his heart.

"Alright. Now get yo ass out my office, I want my damn money back for bailing your ass out too!" Rome joked as Jream smiled in his signature boyish way.

"Put it on my tab old timer." Jream said trying to run out the door.

"I'm gone fuck your little ass up boy!" Rome yelled as the door shut. Jream jogged down the stairs running into Lessiin as he was coming up.

"What you doing here bro?" Jream asked dapping Lessiin up in the process.

"Get out my business Nightmare. But naw I just came to holla at Rome about Emory." Lessiin said continuing his stride up the stairs. Jream shook his head imagining the look on his uncle's face knowing he was losing his top two girls.

Making it back behind the bar, Jream turned his back and started cleaning up and doing his nightly routine. Grabbing a towel to start drying off the glasses, he heard a voice from behind him.

"Excuse me!" the woman yelled over the music getting Jream's attention.

"How can I help you?" Jream turned around throwing the towel over his shoulder

"Can I get two long islands please?" the young woman asked.

"Coming right up." Jream went to work mixing the drink up for her and sat them down.

"That's $6.00." Jream told her as she handed him her card, running he placed the card and receipt down when he heard her say something else.

"Umm can I get a private room with you?" she giggled.

"Nah, but you can get a private room with these hands." Jream's head shot up at the sound of Leylan's voice.

"Girl bye! He fine as the fuck, you should be happy." The woman said. Jream shook his head knowing this wasn't going to end well. When he saw Leylan make a pouty face he knew she was about to be on some other shit. Thinking quickly, he hopped over the bar top and grabbed the front of Leylan's jacket.

"Don't even think about it." He said to her.

"What babe? I was just going to write your fine ass name on her cheek." Leylan said with a sweet facial expression.

"Yeah with a razor, get your ass upstairs crazy." Jream said kissing her on her lips quickly and standing there until she made it hallway to the top before returning behind the bar.

"Humph, stroke game must be bomb!" The woman said switching a little too hard away from the bar. Getting back to his original task, suddenly Jream had a thought and dropped the glass shattering it before jogging towards the stairs and up to his uncle's office.

As soon as his foot hit the top step he saw Lessiin coming from the direction of the restroom and he was trying to read his demeanor, which was like trying to read a brick wall by the way. Lessiin looked Jream up and down

"What the fuck do you do around here? Yo ass aint never behind the bar where you supposed to be." Lessiin said talking shit as usual

"Nigga fuck you, I work. Its Thursday aint shit poppin around this muthafucka but happy hour freaks." Jream said liking that Lessiin wasn't pissed like he thought he would be.

"Makes sense. Well I'm bout to shake, that little nigga Lyberti got us going to Chuckie Cheese's and shit." Lessiin said with a look of disgust written all over his face.

"How my nigga doing man?" Jream said taking a liking to Lyberti on first contact like everyone else. Leylan was obsessed with him so he spent just as much time with them as he did at home.

"Getting on my nerves like everybody else. Between him and Emory always talking, bruh I want to cut my own fucking ears off and burn them bitches with a lighter." Lessiin complained shaking his head. He complained about the noise but missed them when he wasn't near them.

"You'll be alright nigga. I'll see you later, let me go holler at this old nigga right quick." Jream dapped Lessiin up as he headed for the stairs, as soon as he took a step-down, Rome's office door swung open and Leylan voice spilled out of it.

"Thank you for everything Rome. I mean that." Leylan said caught off guard by Jream's uneasy face on the other side of the door.

"Fat Ma what you doing in there?" Lessiin asked coming backup stairs. Rome and Jream looked at each other knowing this wasn't going to be nothing pretty.

"Why you up here?" Leylan challenged back knowing her little secret was coming to a head right before her eyes.

"Y'all come in here and talk" Rome said gesturing with his hands for everyone to come inside his office. Lessiin was the last one to step inside and close the door. Rome sat in his chair, Leylan took a seat on the couch and Jream sat next to her while Lessiin stayed standing with his poker face on full display.

"I'm just going to go ahead and say it, you might be pissed or whatever, but I know you will get over it eventually." Leylan started

"Spit it out." Lessiin said coldly

"Ok, well" Lessiin's phone rang and he almost ignored but glanced down and saw the number from the hospital. Putting up one finger signaling for Leylan to hold on he answered it.

"Yes. Yeah, alright. Let them know we will be there in thirty minutes." Lessiin said in an irritated tone.

"That was Jersey we got to go get Landon, he bout to tear the whole hospital up." All Leylan had to hear was Landon she was already standing to her feet and ready to go about her brother. Piling out the office everyone headed down stairs as Rome gave out orders for everyone in his absence.

"Ride with me" Jream told Leylan and she complied. Her truck would be fine in the lot.

"That was close." Leylan let out the breath she was holding as they sped down the highway keeping up with Lessiin.

"You must pray a lot." Jream said switching lanes.

"Why you say that?" Leylan asked confused

"Because God keeps sparing you. Every time you this close to having to tell your truth, you get out of it." Jream held his hand up showing just how close she had come. He remembered the night Landon and Lessiin were in the club and Leylan suddenly got sick and now he knew why.

"I'm blessed, know that." Leylan said before she laid her head back and gazed out the window. She knew she had to tell her truth soon, she just didn't know the type of backlash she would receive from it.

"Don't get all quiet now Bliss." Jream teased squeezing her thigh as they neared the hospital exit.

"Why you think your brother up here tripping?" Jream asked

"Aint no telling. But I'm about to act a damn fool with him if it's any funny shit going on." Leylan said securing her gun in her waist before they hopped out the car and all walked in the direction of Landon's room

Getting off the elevator they were met by Jersey who looked worried. They could hear Landon's voice from where they were standing and Leylan was about to step right around Jersey and get to her brother. Looking over Jream saw a dark skin nurse laying on a bed with an ice pack being held to their head and blood on their scrubs. He wondered what was going on but tuned into what Jersey was saying.

"I don't know how this happened, I swear it wasn't a joke or anything like that." She plead. Lessiin didn't say a word as he stepped around Jersey politely and headed towards Landon's room. There were two police officers standing outside when they approached who tried to stop them from going in.

"He's pretty irate, we are allowing him some time right now." One of the officers stated "if y'all don't get the fuck out my way. That's our brother." Leylan fussed from behind Jream who gave her a death stare. He had been telling her about her mouth, but she was a work in progress.

"Good luck" one of the officers tried to mumble but Lessiin heard him.

"Who the fuck y'all supposed to be protecting and serving. Y'all over here looking scared as fuck." Shaking his head Lessiin walked around them and went into Landon's room.

"Aye bruh! You bring me some clothes? This the last day I step foot up in this bitch, on God bro!" Landon yelled as he limped around the room

"What happened?" Leylan said concerned and ready

"I told y'all a nigga be high as shit off them pain pills they be giving me, right? So, I'm kicked back and doze off. I swear to God I thought I was having a wet dream because it been a minute or whatever, but the shit start feeling too good so my eyes pop open. Mind you I'm high as giraffe ass, so when I see a head just steadily bobbing on my shit I aint stop the bitch. So, I'm all into it and shit ready to bust down and the muthafucka flips her head to wear I can see her face better and it was TiTi!" Landon explained with a look of pure repulsion on his face.

Leylan, Lessiin, Jream and Jersey who nobody heard come into the room were bent over in laughter. Leylan was red she was laughing so hard. Jream couldn't breath and Lessiin was even amused.

"That shit aint funny! I swear to God punched that nigga so hard three of his teeth were in my lap bruh. I couldn't get to my gun fast enough, so I rolled out that raggedy ass bed and beat his ass with that crutch they gave me. Then Jersey came running her old dramatic ass in here talking bout that's still a woman and I can't be hitting her like that! I started to bop her ass too! I'm ready the fuck to go!" Landon was in true form, he had spit flying everywhere and his chest was heaving up and down as he limped around.

"So, you been up here acting a got damn fool cause an ugly bitch was topping you off?" Lessiin asked egging it on

"I aint with that gay shit Lessiin! That's a fucking boy Damon!" Landon yelled causing Leylan to scream in laughter.

"Jersey are you sure that is a woman?" Lessiin asked her turning serious

"I swear to you she is a woman. But I made sure that I was the only nurse to help Landon while he was here, all other nurses were taken off his charts days ago so I'm not even sure why she was in his room to begin with. Her story is that she was giving Landon a sponge bath and he woke up and attacked her." Jersey said explaining to them what was going on.

"He out there crying and shit, talking about he wants to press charges. That nigga raped me!" Landon said getting madder by the minute.

"Alright calm down nigga. And sit down somewhere. You around here walking around with ya ass all out teasing that nigga and shit." Lessiin said fucking with his brother

"Don't play with me bitch!" Landon said ready to kill Lessiin

"Ok ok calm down. Lessiin leave my brother alone. Landon seriously you have to sit down before you hurt yourself. Jersey can he be discharged now?" Leylan said taking over the situation quickly

"Yes, I have his papers here. He is also banned as of today. They are giving him two hours to his things in order and vacate the premises." Jersey said, trying to control her laughter

"Aint nobody trying to come back to this raggedy piece of shit! I'm calling Fox4 Problem Solvers on y'all too! Got male staff around here fondling the sick and helpless, type of queer ass hospital is this." Landon fussed

"Baby please go get him something to throw on real fast out the gift shop, so we can get him out of here." Leylan asked Jream and he gladly went, his stomach hurt so bad from laughing he needed some air outside that room.

When Jream made it towards the lobby he pulled out his phone seeing he had a text from his roommate and he responded while walking into the gift shop in the hospital. He found a rack with sweatpants and some clearance tee shirts. He grabbed something quick for Landon to throw on and purchased them, so they could go.

When he got back on the floor it had calmed down tremendously, stepping in the room he handed Landon the bag walking back out to give him privacy. Leylan and Lessiin joined him as they sat outside his room laughing about the situation.

While they were talking they saw Loyal walk up and filled him in on what was going on. By the time they got finished Loyal was damn near on the ground crying laughing. As Loyal got himself together the door opened, and Landon came out on his crutch.

"Fuck y'all, out here laughing and shit like I aint a victim." Landon said trying to walk ahead of everyone.

"Landon wait, you have to be taken out by wheelchair, its hospital policy." Jersey told him pushing the wheelchair over his way.

"Bae, you been catering to this nigga?" Loyal joked. He had been developing a bond with his siblings and from the outside looking in you had no way of knowing they all hadn't grown up together.

"I had to keep him out of trouble." Jersey said smiling

"Shit where was you at when that nigga was slobbing on my knob." Landon fussed causing everyone to laugh.

"My woman aint no victim advocate bruh." Loyal joked.

"Lord, why did you give me another annoying brother" Landon said looking up at the sky.

"Who are you staying with Landon?" Leylan asked as they got to the Hospital's exit.

"None of you muthafuckas. Think I'm gone want to hear all that lovey dovey shit all the time. Take. Me. The. Fuck. Home." Landon said with a serious facial expression.

"Landon, you really need to be with someone that can help you at least while you get adjusted to your crutch and cast." Jersey coached.

"Take me to my cousin house then. Sen would never treat a nigga like y'all do." Landon said making Lessiin smack his teeth and finally speak.

"I don't give a fuck where this nigga goes, just come on. Lyberti calling me back to back talking about some damn chuck e cheese." Lessiin complained.

"Ooohh I want to go too" Leylan's childish ass said.

"You can be a kid at home baby" Jream told her whispering in her ear making her giggle.

"Aye Fat Ma, chill out. Shit aint that cool." Fussed as they helped him in the car. Jream was tired for the day and ready to lay down. He didn't feel like driving all the way to Kansas tonight, so he already knew he was crashing at Leylan's. They joked and vibed to the music as they made their way down the highway to Leylan's loft.

Emory

"Come on baby, we have to get some icing for the cakes." Emory said as she and Lyberti walked through Walmart getting some grocery items for dinner.

"No chocolate, like chocolate ugh!" Lyberti scrunched his face up, making Emory laugh and shook her head because he looked just like Lessiin when he did that.

"I like chocolate though. "Emory teased.

"You nasty Em. I like the pink one." Lyberti pointed and Emory grabbed the strawberry icing and put it in the cart. Heading to the back for milk, Lyberti started another conversation with her.

"Em, are you my mama now?" He asked her.

"Why did you ask me that?"

"Cause you act like a mama, you nice and fun." Lyberti said sweetly.

"Was your mama nice and fun too?"

"Umm sometimes, she wasn't nice all the time like you."

"Well look, I'm not trying to take your mommy's place. I'll always be nice and fun, but I want you to remember your mommy because she was there when your daddy couldn't be ok?" Emory didn't really know what to say to him, but she was low key happy that he was fond of her because the feeling was mutual.

"Well aint this some cute shit?" Emory felt a chill run down her back as she heard the voice she had forgotten about come from behind her.

"D-Dez please, not right now. Look I'll give you whatever you think I owe you. just leave me the fuck alone."

"Bitch I – ouch!" Dez looked down at what caused the pain he was experiencing and saw a little boy kicking the shit out of him. Dez pushed Lyberti back making him stumble into Emory who picked him quickly placing him in the basket. Emory turned around quickly punching Dez twice in the face not caring where her fist landed she just needed to distract him a little.

"Argh, I'm gone kill your ass Emory!" Dez tried to wrap his hands around her neck, but as soon as he got a centimeter close he heard someone yelling for help.

"I'm gone get at you!" Dez whispered in a chilling tone before pushing Emory on the ground and taking off out the aisle. The woman that yelled for help ran to her trying to help her up, but the fall had dazed her. Emory was trying to get it together, but the room wouldn't stop spinning.

"Please don't get up, help is coming dear."

"Em!" Lyberti screamed trying to climb out the basket and get to her.

"P-pl Lyberti. M my" Emory couldn't get a full sentence out as she started seeing black spots forming in her vision.

"Coming through. Step back." Paramedics advised as they laid Emory flat on her back trying to assess her injuries.

"My baby…" was the last thing Emory said before she passed out.

***

"Lessiin you're going to wear a hole in the floor, sit down." Seneca fussed as Lessiin paced back and forth in the waiting area. When he got the call that he needed to get to Center Point Medical Center as soon as possible, he thought Landon was being readmitted. But while he was taking his time getting there he got a call from Emory and picked up,

"Aye meet me at Center Point when y'all leave the store." He answered assuming it was Emory

"Pops help! This dude pushed Em down and now she fell asleep!" Lyberti cried into the phone. Lessiin almost crashed, since Lyberti had been in his life he had never once heard him cry. "Where y'all at Lyberti?!"

"We were at the store. Now this lady following the big truck"

"Put the lady on the phone"

"Hello?"

"Who are you?"

"Um I'm Jennifer Fairland, I saw your son's mother fighting with a man and yelled for help. When the guy ran off he pushed her really hard and her head hit the bottom shelf. Your son went ballistic, but he took charge and gave all the information he could. We are following the ambulance now heading to Center Point Medical, do you know where that is?" Jennifer was an older woman with a kind heart, there was no way she was going to keep walking by witnessing the hostile situation that was unfolding in that isle.

"Okay Jennifer listen, I'm ten minutes away." Lessiin was breaking all road laws making highway to his family.

"Here's Lyberti."

"Aye young bull, you good?"

"Yea, pops you coming?" Lyberti had stopped crying and Lessiin was glad, he was doing good with his son, but he still had things to learn when it came to comforting others.

"I'm on my way."

"okay, call me" Lyberti hung up the phone and held on to Emory's purse that he wouldn't let anyone touch. He allowed the EMS worker to get Emory's ID and that was. They were so impressed by Lyberti's knowledge of most of their questions they allowed him to do what he wanted.

That was three hours ago, and nobody had come out to tell them anything. Lessiin was two point five seconds away from murdering the entire staff.

"Excuse me, what the fuck is going on back there? Is she having open heart surgery or what?" Lessiin yelled at the nurse at the desk. She was so frightened that her lips were moving but no words had spilled out.

"Come on." Rocky came over guiding Lessiin away from desk.

"I need answers, what the fuck is going on."

"Bullying these nurses won't get you that either. They know we are out here, when they have everything under control they gone come let us know. Don't break on me Lessiin, this aint even you." Rocky had to in his head because he knew how he felt. If Seneca had been in Emory's place he would probably be ten times worse as Lessiin right now.

"Go check on Lyberti" Lessiin's head shot in the direction of Leylan and Landon who sat holding a conversation with Lyberti as usual. Landon was obsessed with his nephew, he couldn't believe how smart he was, and his demeanor was too cool for a four-year-old.

As if Lyberti could sense his father looking at him he turned around in his chair hopping down with the help of Leylan and ran over holding onto Lessiin by his legs. Lessiin bent down picking him and they stared at each other for a minute before Lyberti wrapped his little arms around Lessiin's neck and laid his head on his shoulder.

Lessiin held on to him walking over to an empty chair sitting down. Lyberti never let up on his embrace and Lessiin didn't either, they were bonding. Leylan had gotten up and snapped pictures of the moment.

"Family of Emory Barth." Lessiin hopped out of his seat with Lyberti still in his arms and stood in front of the doctor.

"Hello. I'm Doctor Simms. Ms. Barth will be just fine. She sustained a minor head injury, in which we did a complete scan and the brain appears to be just fine, no swelling. She suffered a sprained wrist from her fall but other than that everything else is fine. We want to just keep her twenty-four hours to monitor her head over night. You all can see her now. She had been asking for a Lyberti for quite a while now, is that you?" Dr. Simms asked looking at Lessiin who shook his head rolling his eyes a little

"That's me!" Lyberti answered popping his head off his father's shoulder for a second for the introduction.

"Well nice to meet you. Are you ready to go see mom?"

"She left. But I want to see Em please." Lyberti said with wide eye looking around the doctor.

"Well follow me."

"Come on pops!"

"You can't walk now?"

"I'm cool up here." Lyberti laid his head back down and everybody laughed at his response as Lessiin lead the way following behind Dr. Simms to Emory's room.

When the door opened, it seemed like everyone let out a sigh of relief when they laid eyes on Emory who was sitting up smiling. They really didn't know what to expect but they were happy to know that she looked like her normal self.

"Em!" Lyberti yelled trying to squirm out of Lessiin's arms now.

"Oh, now ya little ass want to get down." Lyberti climbed in the bed with Emory and they hugged like long lost best friends.

"Em I missed you!"

"I missed you too! I'm sorry I scared you, but I heard you had my back." Emory held her left fist up and Lyberti gave her a pound and they laughed.

"Y'all two are sickening" Leylan joked walking over to the bed to give Emory a hug, "I'm so happy you are alright. Heard you got a mean two piece too." Leylan winked at Lyberti and they laughed.

"Yo sis! You had a nigga shook for a minute, but I'm glad your pint size ass is ok." Landon told her slowly making his way over to the bed with his crutches

"Keep talking and I'm gone het nurse Johnson up here."

"See you shot the fuck out for that" Landon's body shook as he cringed

"That boy is rotten." Seneca said shaking her head and drawing everyone's attention to a now knocked out Lyberti. He had curled up in Emory's side and fell right to sleep.

"You would have sworn she birthed him, y'all heard Ms. Jennifer say how he ran up on dude." Landon shook his head imaging the scene

"Speaking of, who was he Emory?" Rocky asked ready to body whoever. Everyone in that room was family so all violations against them were punishable by death in his eyes and he was ready to be the grim reaper.

Lessiin hadn't said a word since they had been in the room, but he was right by Emory's side. She felt the love radiating off him and everyone could feel it in the atmosphere. Everybody in that hospital room knew Lessiin, so his antics didn't surprise any of them.

"Leylan do you remember the guy Dez I told you about?" Emory asked as Leylan's body went stiff. She was angry.

"The nigga I bow wowed at the store?" Lessiin finally spoke. When Emory shook her head confirming what he said he nodded his head and looked directly at Leylan and Landon who started their triplet communication.

"He just wants that money. At this point he can have the shit, so I can have my peace of mind." Emory sighed shaking her head

"Like the fuck you will! Fuck that nigga and any bread he thinks he entitled to. Aint like he gone be breathing long enough to spend the shit, he fucked up when he hurt you, but he murdered himself when he touched my nephew." Leylan sassed ready to boot up, her thirst for blood was aching and she needed a release.

"We gone get out of here and let you rest baby girl. Rocky grab ya boy he is coming with us, so they can relax." Seneca ordered

"Aww you don't have to take him." Emory said as Rocky picked Lyberti up throwing him over his shoulder. He was dead to the world.

"Child bye! Your baby will be back once you get settled."

"Yeah Em damn, I got to get this little nigga in training anyway." Landon threw fake jabs at a sleeping Lyberti.

"Good night y'all." Leylan said hugging everybody and kissing Lyberti on the cheek. Everyone started clearing out the room leaving Emory and Lessiin.

"Come here." Emory lifted the sheet the draped over her inviting Lessiin in the bed. He slowly walked over sitting on the edge but not laying back. Emory laid her head on his shoulder and they sat in silence not saying anything. The only thing that could be heard in the room was the air coming through the vents.

"You love me, huh?" Emory said breaking the silence.

"You coo."

"I love you too" Emory kissed the back of Lessiin's neck and laid back in the hospital bed ready to close her eyes. She felt the shift in the bed and felt Lessiin's arm wraparound her and she was at peace as they both dosed off content.

Nefe

Stepping out of her shoes as she took a deep breath glad to be home after a long day. Nefe walked into her living room placing her purse on the ottoman, turning around she screeched and dropped her phone on the floor.

"Why are you here?" she said breathless still trying to regain her composure.

"You know why I'm here."

"If anything happens to me they will know it was you."

"But can they prove it, is the question. Come on ma, you know what's up. I mean after all you were my first love and all."

"Are you going to let me explain and you just here to do what you have to do. You killing me won't stop shit by the way." Nefe figured if she through that little bit of info in there it would help her case, but deep down she honestly knew it wouldn't. She just wanted to prolong the inevitable.

"Mhm mph m, come of Nefe stop it. Now sit yo ass down!"

"How's Lyberti?"

"Fine"

"Does he ask about me?"

"Not so much anymore."

"I figured. When had him, I knew he was going to be a genius. The doctors were so fascinated by the day-old baby that stayed awake for hours on end and held his head up after only being in the world a few hours. He would respond to my voice too, I could be clear across the room talking and he would shift his eyes trying to locate me. I hated that he looked so much like you and your family." Nefe had tears rolling down her face as she spoke. Unfazed Lessiin let her get it out anyway.

"That was a sign. You were dead ass wrong for keeping him away from us, no fuck that me! I've been thinking about how I wanted to dismember you, torture you and some more shit. But even your dog ass doesn't deserve that quick death. I was going to let you live even, you would never see my son again, but you could have still been alive." Lessiin twirled hunting knife in his hand as talked looking straight ahead.

"Oh yeah, why the change of heart then?"

"Ha-ha!"

"Ahhh arghhh fuck!" Nefe bent over in pain as the knife penetrated her knee, she wanted to pull it out, but the pain was too great.

"Don't keep fucking with me. And give me mishit back" Lessiin stood up slowly walking towards her. He saw that she wasn't moving to take the knife out of her knee, so he decided to help her.

Nefe was normally feisty as hell, Lessiin knew this kill was going to be all over the place because she would try to fight it. Surprisingly she wasn't. Lessiin bent down slightly bringing himself eye level to her and gripped the knife. Instead of just pulling it straight out he turned it at the same time he pulled, causing her to scream out.

"Now, what you're going to do is get up and take me to the video's." Lessiin knew Nefe just as well as he knew himself, he knew her whole house was under surveillance and she had them stored around there somewhere.

Getting up slowly, Nefe limped towards the stairs. Looking at all of them she shook her head and started up slowly. When she got to the picture on the wall she stopped. Lessiin slapped her on the back of head

"Don't try it Nefe. You forgot I damn near raised you, keep it moving." Nefe had guns stashed around the entire house, just like Lessiin. They were in the weirdest places but convenient for the owner to get to when needed.

Nefe finally made it up the stairs and lead Lessiin to a door that a big red car on the front. Lessiin figured it was Lyberti's room but he didn't say anything as Nefe opened the door. She limped over to the closet and pushed a button that turned the clothes that hung inside around. Lessiin was really impressed by what he was seeing.

The closet lead to another room that had about size screens mounted on the wall, you could see the entire house and the perimeter outside from those six screens. Nefe sniffled as she hit a few buttons on a keyboard and a disc popped out, next all six screens read powering down until they went black. Nefe started to shake because she knew her time on this earth was winding down slowly.

Lessiin grabbed the disc and put it in his hoodie pocket before he turned to walkout the closet. Nefe slowly followed and looked around Lyberti's room. Her precious baby boy would never be seeing her face again. She wouldn't get to see him grow older, she wouldn't be seeing him ride his bike without training wheels, driving for the first time, going off to prom, nothing.

For the first time in a long time Nefe started praying. She prayed that Lessiin would raise their child to be better than the both of them, she prayed that when Lessiin told him stories of her they he would try to keep them on a positive note as not to tarnish the small amount of time they shared together.

"You remember when we got that apartment off Armor." Lessiin asked her as he picked up pictures and toys that belonged to Lyberti. Nefe chuckled and sniffled at the thought

"New Jack City is what we called it. We spent our food money for that week trying to buy traps and cleaning supplies."

"When did you turn rat Nefe?" Lessiin wanted to know, no he needed to know. Nefe was there from the start, shit if Lessiin wasn't so worried about keeping her sheltered she would have been a damn assassin.

Nefe had it rough as a kid, she was never really a kid. One of her mother's little brother snuck into her bedroom every night from age eleven until about fourteen. He was only six years older than Nefe and told her they were playing house. Once Nefe started learning in school what playing house really was, she threatened to tell and her Uncle, in true fuckboy fashion threatened her.

Their whole family adored her uncle so Nefe figured they wouldn't believe a word she said. Molestation and rape was like a taboo in their black family up brining. One-day Nefe sat at Gillham park swinging on the play set when she saw a boy watching two other kids play with a ball. They all looked around the same age and they were having a good time.

Nefe walked over to the boy who was sitting at the bottom of the slide and spoke to him. He didn't say anything, he didn't turn his faceup or anything, he just looked. Nefe started a one-sided conversation with him and he appeared to be listening just not responding. When Nefe realized she was babbling she turned to walk away when he finally said something.

"What's your name?"

"I'm Nefetaria. What's your name?"

"Lessiin."

"Nice to meet you. How old are you?"

"14."

"Oh, me too! I just turned 14 though. Why you just sitting here by yourself?"

"I'm chilling, my brother and sister came down here and I'm just looking out."

"Ok cool. Well nice meeting you Lessiin, I'm leaving now." Nefe said turning to walk away

"You gone be at school tomorrow?"

"Y-yeah. What school you go to?"

"Same school as you, duh."

"I never seen you before. You see me?"

Lessiin just nodded his head in response. Nefe waived her hand and skipped off, she was happy he had noticed her and now she was going to be paying more attention. After that day Nefe and Lessiin hardly were ever seen without the other. Aside from Leylan and Landon you never saw him without one of the three.

That's why deep down Lessiin was really hurt by Nefe's betrayal. She had it made, from the lowest of lows to the highest of highs Lessiin always made sure she was taken care of. He may have slacked off on spending time with her at times, but that's small shit that could have been addressed.

Zoning back into the conversation at hand Lessiin stared at Nefe intensely.

"I didn't want to." She said barely above a whisper.

"Speak up! Don't start that whispering shit now!" Lessiin yelled at her

"I didn't have a choice! He had me cornered and it was y'all or me!" Nefe screamed

"Who? Who the fuck had you so shook that you turned rat?"

"Feliz!"

Cocking his gun that Nefe never saw him produce, Lessiin was getting frustrated trying to pull the information out of Nefe so he was ready to shoot the shit out of her.

"How. The. Fuck. Did. It. Happen." Lessiin said his words slowly and clearly fed up by this scene.

"You remember my uncle that I told you about when we were kids?"

"The one you wouldn't tell me his name? Yeah, I remember, but we done with that reminiscing shit Nefe. I'm telling you stop stalling and spit that shutout!"

"Feliz is the uncle that wouldn't stop touching me! He told me that if I didn't help him, he would tell my whole family how I was a whore and kept trying to throw myself on him. They would have believed him too, he was golden boy." Nefe's shoulders shook as she released years of pain and heartache.

She had been living the Alexander nightmare he whole life. When she left Lessiin, she wasn't running from him threatening her about cheating, she called herself escaping. She thought she finally freed herself of the torture. About two weeks after finding out she was pregnant, she decided she was going to sneak back into town and let Lessiin know about the baby.

The first night she punked out. She had made it as far as getting dressed but when she turned the door knob to walkout her hotel room, she freaked out. She needed to rehearse what she would say. She already knew the baby belonged to Lessiin by what the doctor told her, so that wasn't what had her terrified.

She planned to tell Lessiin everything, from the plan of the feds to the baby and all. On the second day she finally made it out the hotel room. She knew Lessiin like the back of her hand, so she knew exactly where he would be. She pulled up to 24 Hour Fitness and got a parking spot right in the front of the building. Just like she had suspected Lessiin could be seen on the basketball court playing ball with his brother.

Just as she stepped out of her car she felt the pressure of someone grabbing her arm.

"Shut up, and lets go."

Nefe's knees buckled at the sound of his voice, she could have kicked her own ass for being caught slipping this way. She knew better. As they made it to the ford F-150 truck she hopped in and stayed close to the door, she was prepared to tuck and roll to get away from this muthafucka if she had too.

"Where you been niecey pooh?"

"On vacation"

"That's cute. But why didn't you tell us, my sister has been worried about you girl."

"Cut the shit Feliz. I'm grown as fuck, what do you want?" Nefe had no respect for his bitch ass what so ever. If she could get away with it, she would shoot him right between the eyes and piss on his grave every chance she got.

"You right, but you work for me. You have a job to do. Or I can just tell your little boyfriend in there how you turned informant to keep from going to jail. We know your spoiled ass wouldn't make it twelve full hours locked up." Feliz spat with vindication.

"I need some time! Fuck he just found out I was cheating on him, I left to make it look like I was hurt and then I would come back and win him back. You don't know him like I do, I need you to get off my fucking back and let me handle this how I see fit!" Nefe lied through her teeth.

"Ok, ok take your little vacation then, but you need to call my sister. She really is worried about you."

"Yeah I bet." Nefe reached for the door handle but Feliz stopped her.

"What were you about to do though?"

"I was going to give him his key back to his house real dramatic like. But you fucked up my entrance" Nefe rolled her eyes and hopped out of his truck. As she made her way to her car she thought how close she had come to being busted and decided she was going to do what she did best; run.

"That's bullshit!" Lessiin let off a shot missing her head by two inches on purpose.

"Lessiin!" Nefe had peed her pants

"Get your pissy ass up! Gone pee on your damn self, if I wanted you dead you'd be stinking already! Get the fuck up and let's go!" Lessiin walked by the door and stood there waiting for her to get up.

"Where—"

"Shut the fuck up, don't ask me shit, just follow directions. Go clean yourself up now and meet me right back here, you got fifteen minutes" Lessiin stood in the door way allowing her to scurry off towards her bedroom to get cleaned up.

Nefe thought her prayers may have worked, because true indeed, if Lessiin wanted her dead she would damn sure wouldn't be amongst the land of the living right now. She just wondered what he was about to do with her.

Landon

"Aye turn on the news!"

"Really?!"

"My bad, but turn that shit on, hurry up!" Landon was hype and they wanted to know why.

"Reporting live from Raymore, Missouri a quadruple homicide; tonight, police tell us that there were four victims found inside this home in the normally quite suburb. This house roped off behind me is where investigators are saying they have found the bodies of Lieutenant Alexander, his wife Simone Alexander, Twenty-nine-year-old Richard Watts and his wife Leslie Watts. The cause of death has not been released yet, but we are told by the witness who found the two couples inside 'it was something out of horror film'. We will be reporting on this story as it develops. Back to –"

"Y'all see that shit?!" Landon said hype

"Sit your ass down before you go into remission" Seneca fussed, "And get out we will be down in a minute, get Ed and Eddy's asses over here now."

"Ugh Sen, you naked under there? Let me find out Rocky was in here doing the rock away" Landon ducked as a house shoe came flying his way.

"Get out lil nigga" Rocky laughed as he made faces inciting Seneca who was trying to go catch him.

Landon pulled out his phone and Facetime'd Lessiin first and got no answer. That was strange because Lessiin never missed a phone call from his siblings. He chalked it up to the reception in the hospital being bad. Sending him a text in code, Landon FaceTimed Leylan next.

"Sup?" Jream answered once the phone connected

"Boy if you don't get yo 'you don't want no problems wit me' Chance the Rapper looking ass off my sister phone." Landon didn't care who you were or what time of day it was, you were catching these jokes.

"Not too much on bae" Leylan said in the background

"I'm gone stomp on that nigga bad foot baby, don't even worry about it." Jream flipped Landon off and handed the phone Leylan.

"What you want dude?"

"Aye Fat Ma, I'm scarred for life sis on baby nem."

"What, what happened, do I need to pull up?" Leylan was TTG (Trained To Go) when it came to her brothers and especially Landon. The triplets all had a bond, but Leylan and Landon were especially closer. The two of them were the girl and boy version of the other really.

"Yeah you do. But, when you get here I'm gone tell you why. Let me tell you what scarred me though; I walked in the room like I always do but this time Rocky and Sen was tryna coverup and shit. I think Rocky was deep sea diving my nigga."

Leylan was in tears laughing at her brother, he was a damn fool.

"No, for real you need to turn your TV on and then make it here ASAP." Landon got serious as he watched his sister's eye's get big looking at her TV She didn't say a word as the call disconnected and Landon knew she was on her way.

Making his way down the hallway he stopped and checked in on Lyberti who was knocked out as he should be. Landon was a night owl, so Lyberti thought he could be too. They were up until four in the morning, but the difference between the two was that Landon only needed a few hours of sleep before he was right back up ready to get shit poppin. Little Lyberti wasn't about that life.

It would take about twenty to thirty minutes before everybody arrived at the house, so he just sat down and turned the tv up switching to all the different news outlets talking about the gruesome homicide of the Lieutenant and his wife and friends.

Landon's mind drifted off to Essynce, some days he wanted to go hunt her down and skin her alive. Then other days he sat back and thought about the reason why she was going to do what she was going to do. Maybe she didn't have a choice. That was when Landon was sober though, like now. He yearned to hear her voice again and explain herself, he saw himself with Essynce that what hurt him the most. He was ready to settle down and she would have been the pick of the litter.

Picking up his phone Landon hopped on Facebook to see what people were talking about. He saw he had six new inbox messages and contemplated if he feltlike having conversation today. Deciding he would check them later, he scrolled through his notifications stopping in his tracts at what he saw.

The crazy bitch Taliyah had uploaded a picture. Landon saw that she hadn't taken her location off when she posted it talking about "I'm Back" so he screenshot it for future references, when they were done dealing with all this other shit. Taliyah was dead on site. As if a lightbulb went off in his head he called Loyal.

"I don't want to hear none of that funny shit." Loyal answered exhaling the smoke he was holding.

"Come fire up with yo big bro, we about to have a meeting at Sen's anyway." Landon was bonding with Loyal and he loved the kid.

"Another meeting? Y'all talk too much. Send me ya location." Loyal complained but he was happy deep down that they were even including him in on family business.

"Ol Khalid ass nigga" Landon laughed and hung up before Loyal got started. That nigga could hang with Landon with the jokes and they would go at it for hours. Sending his location, he got up to outside and fire up. Lyberti's door was open so he must have been in the kitchen or bathroom.

"Unca Lan you going outside?" Landon heard his little voice as soon as he hit the door.

"Yep, go put your house shoe on if you coming dude."

"Nope! Go was your hands so you can eat breakfast. You don't need to go outside with him, unless you are smoking now?" Seneca gave Lyberti a hard look. He busted out laughing and shook his head no while running to wash his hands.

"He can't be around y'all with everything y'all do. He is a child." Seneca fussed

"That's my protégé, he gotta see how he supposed to be rocking when he gets my age."

"Boy bye. You want oatmeal too?"

"For sure! You know how I like it."

Seneca nodded her head as she went to prepare breakfast for her family. When Landon stepped into the closed in deck that Rocky had built onto the house for times like these, Landon went straight to his favorite spot and sat down. He started rolling his blunt and got ready to spark it when it was snatched out of his mouth.

"Aye what the fuck! Boy you better make some noise round this bitch, almost got ya ass popped!"

"You wasn't gone do shit, slow ass."

"Yo whole shit was gone be blew back" Landon pointed down at the desert eagle he had in his right hand

"Good shit grass hopper. Now light up" Lessiin teased tossing the blunt back in Landon's lap and pulling out his own supply to roll.

"Don't start without ya girl" Leylan's loud ass came out followed by Jream and Jersey

"How all y'all get here when the weed come out, ga damn coons" Landon joked as he lit his blunt and started the session.

"New York, where my brother?"

"Nigga get cut. Lyberti was showing him the new game y'all got him, knowing Loyal he in there showing him all the secret codes and shit to cheat." Jersey joked

"That nigga too damn smart." Lessiin commented passing his blunt to Leylan.

"Jersey, you smoke?" Leylan asked

"Only with Loyal sometimes."

"Smart girl. But you good with us too." Lessiin responded. He had good vibes from Jersey, so he was talkative and cordial with her.

"He likes you." Landon joked seeing that Lessiin vibed with Jersey. Anybody else would have been getting the stare down and grilled by now.

"I passed the test then." Jersey joked as everybody including Lessiin laughed at her fake wiping sweat off her forehead. Loyal joined them and the session was under way. Shortly after Rocky came out and opened the deck up. It was a nice day for it to be December, so the clan was taking advantage of it. Seneca started bringing the breakfast out and setting it up like a buffet style, so everyone could pick they wanted. It was clear everyone had the munchies at this point so when Lessiin sat Lyberti down with his plate everybody swarmed the table like vultures.

"High asses" Seneca joked sitting next to Lyberti while they ate and held conversation.

"Pops, where is Em?" Lyberti asked with a mouth full of eggs

"Big Bro bringing her, she should be pulling up. And stop talking with your mouth full."

"Sen! Landon taking all the apples out the oatmeal!" Leylan told pouting.

"I cut some extra apples up, they in there on the island Fat Ma."

"Baby, bring me some more milk too please." Jream asked as she walked into the house.

"Me too baby!" Lyberti yelled.

"Aye lil nigga, that's my woman watch out." Jream and Lyberti started play fighting while Landon recorded. The vibes were on point, if only for a little while.

"Aye Jream my young bull was working you out" Lessiin boasted.

"Lil nigga got a mean right hook" Jream complimented and ruffled Lyberti's dreads at the same time.

"Look who I found?" Leylan announced as she and Emory stepped out on the deck.

"Em!" Lyberti jumped out his chair running at her full speed

"Stop running" everybody said at the same time and laughed

"Y'all all high." Emory commented bending down to hug Lyberti and making her way to greet everybody.

"Okay lil boy, go inside and play in your room while the grown folks talk." Seneca instructed. In true dramatic fashion Lyberti had to stall by going to everybody individually to tell them he would see them later.

"That's that Landon rubbing off on him." Rocky said laughing

"I told y'all that's my protégé" he boasted

"So, I'm assuming everybody has seen or heard the news?" Rocky started their meeting

"Fill me in." Lessiin put his blunt out and sat up

"Lieutenant Alexander is no longer amongst the living" Rocky said with pride, "Along with his wife and friends. So, I say that to say this, Trips y'all already know what's to come with this. Educate your spouses and everyone move accordingly. We are alert at all times, as y'all know this started the war." Rocky looked his family in the eyes.

"War? What's up, put the kid on game." Loyal spoke up feeling lost.

"Every single last one of us will be asked for our alibi, so be prepared for visits from our boys in blue. Nobody is to speak to them, we let Finelley do the talking. Y'all have nothing to worry about, after all none of us in *this* room had anything to do with it."

"But a Miahgo did?" Lessiin lifted his eyebrow saying what everyone was thinking. They all knew each others MO and that massacre had Miahgo all over it.

"Like I was saying, Loyal you and Jersey have nothing to worry about. Just know that your last name holds major weight and hate. The whole town is a suspect right now but the Miahgo's are numero Uno."

"Jersey and Emory, I need y'all to go check on Lyberti." Emory looked at Lessiin sideways but got up anyway. Jersey didn't care either way, so she got up with no problem and headed inside. Once the ladies were in the house Lessiin began talking

"Last night, I snatched Nefe. She is in the warehouse."

"Why is she still breathing?" Leylan knew her brother and she knew he was stalling Nefe out, but why?

"Don't let her get in your head bro." Landon could see the confliction in his eyes.

"That's not it" Lessiin slammed his hand on the table

"Why are you so defensive then? We know you better than you give us credit for! You are stalling that bitch out because she is your baby mama and you feel sorry for her. We see how this shit is about to go!" Leylan didn't give a fuck about Nefe being her nephews mother. All rats must die in her eyes. Nefe didn't give a fuck when she was working with the feds against them.

"Y'all listen before you start assuming." Seneca jumped in wondering why Lessiin locked Nefe up instead of deading her.

"That's the thing; I don't have to explain shit. I was respectful enough to let y'all know what was going on, I didn't have too."

"Nigga you got us fucked up! We a team! You aint Lessiin the one man show! If I had done the same thing with Essynce you would have had a fucking problem with it."

"You don't even know that bitch!"

"Neither do you! Obviously!" Landon and Lessiin were in a face off in each other's face. They both were huffing and puffing, and the tension was thick.

"Everybody calm down."

"I am calm. I'm just sick of this emotionally detached shit this nigga be on. We are triplets, we cooked together, and everything we do is together! That's all I'm saying. If you want that rat bitch in your life, fine! Fuck it then, but don't play us with that I don't have to tell y'all shit. I'm out." Landon grabbed his crutches and left the deck headed to his own house. He needed a break from everybody.

Leylan didn't say a word as she gathered her stuff, she walked over and hugged Rocky and Seneca. She bent down and hugged Loyal before leaving without acknowledging Lessiin.

"Y'all call me." Loyal stated before saying his goodbyes and grabbing Jersey before they left.

"You know what you need to do youngin." Rocky helped Seneca up and left Lessiin to his own thoughts. Lessiin plopped down in his chair and let his dreads fall to the front while he put his head in his hands. He felt like somebody was staring at him, so he looked up to find Emory standing there with a tear stained face, she had heard the entire argument.

She knew Lessiin still held feelings for his baby mama and that hurt. When he left the hospital the other night to 'handle business' she hadn't heard from him again until that morning when he told her Big Bo was picking her up.

Emory shook her head and turned to leave. Lessiin didn't even get up to try and stop her, he knew he was wrong. How the fuck did he become the enemy, was the question swarming Lessiin's mind.

Feliz

"You still haven't heard from her?"

"No, didn't I tell you I would let you know if I did?" Feliz fussed at his worrisome sister asking about her daughter

"Don't get snappy with me Feliz, I just asked you a question. We all are mourning and hurt and lost. I just want my child here with me." She cried

"I'm sorry Nissa, I'm just in a different head space right now. I've been calling Nefe all morning, I don't know where she could be." In all actuality Feliz could give a shit where his niece was right now. His twin the one he shared everything with, was gone. He was murdered savagely, and he knew exactly who to point the finger at. But there was no proof, the investigators said they had never seen anything like it.

When the coroner had to come and get the bodies, even he got sick at the scene. Feliz went into the basement of his sister's home so he could have some alone time. He couldn't think straight with all the crying and people stopping by. Half of them were truly saddened and the others were just downright nosey trying to get the scoop.

This was the biggest massacre the city had seen in years. The lieutenant of the Federal Bureau of Investigations, murdered in his own home along with his wife and friends. Feliz pulled the bottle of vodka he had in his pocket out and unscrewed the top. Taking the bottle to the head he drank it like it was tap water.

"Ahhhh. Damn Felix, how am I supposed to go on without you bro?" Feliz was sick to his stomach with grief. As the liquor started coursing through his body, Feliz started thinking more and more. He wanted revenge badly, but without his twin he didn't know which way was up. That family had destroyed them, they had been a pain in the ass for years. Just when they thought they were getting lead way on diminishing the notorious family, they were always ten steps ahead of them.

"Feliz. Feliz are you down here?" Nissa called out

"Yeah?!"

"Come quick, please! Hurry!" Nissa was frantic as Feliz rushed upstairs to see what the problem was now.

"This was on the porch, so I opened it. Who would do this?! Can't you do something?!" Nissa screamed in hysteria.

Feliz walked over to the table to look at what had his sister so shaken. Wishing he hadn't he stepped back and vomited all over the floor. Everything that Feliz had in his insides was now on the kitchen floor as he shook his head at what he had just witnessed in that box.

"Get it out of here!" Nissa screamed on the verge of passing out, she couldn't take anymore

"Anderson come to my sister's place now! Stop, drop what you are doing and get here NOW!" Feliz screamed into his phone. Staggering to the sink he grabbed two of Nissa's decorative towels and through one over the box and the other over the vomit he spilled on the floor.

Pulling the vodka out of his pocket again, he turned the bottle up finishing it off.

"Are you serious right now? Feliz what the hell is going on out in them streets? First my daughter runs off and comes back with a child, now my baby brother and his wife have been savagely murdered, and your ass is in here drinking like a damn fish!"

"What you trying to say Nissa?! Huh? You act like I did this shit, I lost my brother too, my got damn twin at that. I don't know about your fucking daughter, that's your job!"

"Now you wait one fucking minute Feliz Nathaniel Alexander, what you will do is show me respect! I raised your nappy headed ass and you won't sit here and disrespect me in my damn home! I asked you a sensible amount of questions, I didn't blame you for shit, unless your feeling guilty?" Nissa bucked right back at her younger brother. It was her who raised the twins when their parents died in a tragic car accident. She was a child raising children, but she made it work, even when she slipped and got pregnant with Nefe, she still maintained in raising them all.

"Look Nissa, I need you to get off my back, alright? I'm dealing with enough shit from work and now this, I don't need your overbearing nature on top of that."

"Overbearing nature? Nigga my brother is dead, and my child is missing, I'm not over bearing, I'm concerned. Speaking of which; where is your wife?" Nissa turned her nose up like shit stunk in the air. Feliz had to agree with her, where the hell was Elise?

Walking past his sister he headed back down to the basement for some privacy, pulling out his phone he called Elise twice before she picked up the third time. Not giving her a chance to say hello, he ripped into her

"Where the fuck are you at? Now is not the time to be pulling your bullshit Elise!" Feliz had switched the phone to speaker so he could look for some more liquor in the cabinets down there.

"Oh, is that anyway to talk to your wife?"

"Where is Elise and who the fuck is this?"

"I'm hurt, you don't remember my voice? Come on old friend try one more time."

"I'll kill you bitch! What did you do to my wife?!" Feliz had spit spraying everywhere as he yelled into the phone once realization sat in.

"Let's trade, shall we? You come to your house now and I'll let Elise go in exchange for you? Sound good?"

"You bitch! I thought it was 'no women or kids' or did the game change?"

"Don't try to play me bitch nigga. I know we aren't talking about rules, when incest seems to be your thing."

"I'll be there in an hour" Feliz said quickly, disconnecting the call.

"Incest? What is going on Feliz? Who was that?" Nissa had caught the very end of the conversation once she heard the yelling she came down to check on her brother and heard that.

"What did I just say upstairs Nissa?! I got to go though, Elise needs me. Dont open the door once I leave, if people want to leave shit tell them to take everything to the church and you need some alone time right now. Nissa listen to me; Do not open the door for anybody."

"Ok your scaring me, am I in danger? What the fuck is going on?!"

"Just do what I said!" Feliz rushed past her up the stairs and right into Anderson, on edge Feliz whipped out his gun and almost fired it.

"Announce yourself next time, you almost died today!"

"I had been banging on the door sir, nobody answered so I came in" Anderson stammered

"I need you to take that box to the coroner and find out what I believe I already know."

"What is it. Oh shit!" Anderson jumped back when he removed the towel off the top of the box.

"I think it's the lieutenants."

"Is this a joke?" Anderson wanted to be sure, he had never seen no shit like this

"Am I laughing? It was left on the porch, get it to the coroner asap!"

"Who would take the time to cut somebody's heart and tongue out and put it in a box, sir this is some sick shit."

"Tell me something I don't know." Feliz walked past Anderson and his sister that stood there scolding him and headed to his home to rescue his wife.

***

"Can I just go?"

"You can sit the fuck down, like I told you to"

"No need to be rude Thiago, after all we do have history."

"Bitch you sucked my dick when were sixteen, after history class. Now sit the fuck down before I shoot you in your knee." Thiago could have shot himself the way Elise was working his nerve. Cesare better be lucky they were good friends and Thiago owed him a favor.

"As soon as your husband gets here, you can go. Until then shut the fuck up and try to sit and look pretty." Looking at the clock on the wall, Feliz had twenty-five minutes to be pulling in the driveway. There was no doubt in Thiago's mind that Feliz would beat the clock and be there in less time.

Thiago never understood what they saw in Elise, but her pussy must leak gold. I mean why else would Feliz turn around and marry her after she fucked his best friend, got married to him, had three kids by him and then ran back to his dumbass leaving the kids with Renzo. That was some shit you read about in a K.C. Mills book. But Feliz surely thought he had a dime on his arm but that bitch wasn't even worth a wooden nickel in Thiago's eyes.

From the time she came home and realized he was in her house, she had been trying to throw her ass at him. Thiago thought she was going to rape him at one point. That's why it took so long for him to answer the phone when Feliz called, he was fighting her off his pants.

"Have you talked to Renzo?" Elise asked trying to figure out who she would run to now since she just knew Feliz was as good as dead.

"Why?"

"I mean he is my baby daddy and ex-husband. A girl can ask, can't she?"

"Bitch please, but if you must know Renzo is dead." Thiago hated saying that. Him and Renzo had formed a bond outside of business, Thiago's kids loved Renzo's and vice versa.

"What?! How?! Why didn't anybody tell me?"

"Don't start that fake crying shit. Tell you for what?"

"Where are my kids?"

"What kids? You gave up your rights three years ago, them kids don't even acknowledge you!"

"You act like I had a choice! He would have never let me leave with them! I had to run off."

"Type of shit you on ma? I dont know about you and Renzo's personal shit and I don't care to. But I will say this, you should have been a better mother and woman, no real woman runs off leaving her kids to re-marry shortly after and never try to gain some kind of contact. I ain't buying it, so sell that shit to somebody else." Thiago leaned back in is seat watching the clock that he swore had to be broken.

"You don't know shit! Fuck you Thiago!"

"I wouldn't fuck you with Usher's dick ma'am, now shut the fuck up"

Elise crossed her arms and sat back pouting immaturely. As if God read Thiago's thoughts, Feliz car came zooming into the driveway as he stumbled out.

"Elise! Elise! Elise baby I'm here!" Feliz was drunk as hell

"In here honey! Thank god you came he was trying to rape me!"

"Bitch, I'll knock all thirty-two of them teeth out your noggin, don't disrespect me or my dick like that!" Thiago had had enough of this circus act. Pulling out the needle he had in his pocket he walked over to Feliz and Elise and stuck them both in the neck and waited for the effects of the serum to kick in, which only took about thirty seconds.

"Nigga consider all debts re-payed! We on the way"

"Was it that bad?"

"That bad? I almost poked my damn self with this shit"

"I appreciate ya"

"Say less Cesare." Thiago ended the call and called in his team to move the two clowns to their next destination.

Essynce

"It's been three weeks and the search continues for Chief Alexander and Nefetaria Miles. There have been no leads in the case. Investigators are asking the community for any help or tips to bring these two home. This is in lieu of the horrendous murder of the FBI's Lieutenant Alexander, also a relative of Miles and Alexander which remains unsolved. If you have any information regarding these cases, please call 1-800-TIPS and you will remain anonymous. Back to you in the studio Brian"

Pacing back and forth Essynce was a nervous wreck. Every time she heard the reports on the news her anxiety shot through the roof. Most of her wounds had healed to perfection and her arm was only in a sling instead of a full-blown cast. Essynce had left her parents home and had been staying back at her own place with her best friend as a new roommate.

"E, do you want to go with me to the mall?" Naomi peeked her head in the doorway to ask her.

"Nah, thanks though."

"You need to. Its not healthy for you to be cooped up in the house twenty-four seven. I'm only going to a few stores, we'll be there an hour tops."

"Ok. Ok, fine I'll go." Essynce walked over to her closet to find something decent to wear considering it was a Friday and there would be a lot of people at the mall. Deciding on a gray Puma Fenty set and matching Fenty creepers, Essynce went into her bathroom and looked in the mirror. Thank God, she didn't look like she felt or had been through. She sprayed her hair with a conditioner and water mix and left it in its natural curly state placing a side part on the right side.

Going back in her room to get dressed it only took her about twenty minutes to be presentable and Naomi was ready and waiting for her in the living room.

"Cute bitch!"

"Thank you, I aint feeling it though. But whatever." Essynce through her crossbody bag over her shoulder and followed Naomi out to the car. They sang and joked all the way to the mall, making Essynce feel a little better already. She hadn't been out in a while, so the sun was doing her some justice.

Making it inside the mall the girls hit their favorite store first, Forever 21. Browsing the racks looking for nothing, Essynce wasn't paying attention when she bumped into a fine specimen of a man.

"My bad ma."

"Its fine, I wasn't looking, excuse me." Essynce stepped around him trying to find Naomi in the busy and cluttered store.

"I didn't catch your name."

"I didn't pitch it" Essynce rolled her eyes

"Damn like that, I wasn't gone spit no weak ass game or nothing like that miss." Essynce had to crack smile at that, because there was no doubt in her mind that he would be trying to spit some game.

"What happened to your arm?"

"Car wreck."

"Damn muthafuckas in KC can't drive"

"Where you from?"

"I'm from here, but I moved out to California and live there now."

"I've never been to Cali before, how do you like it?"

"Enough to only comeback when needed and nothing more." They both laughed

"I'm Rumi though."

"Essynce"

"That's what's up. Aye look it was nice running into you ma. Keep your head up, I got to make moves." Rumi winked and walked away leaving Essynce drooling at his cool ass demeanor.

"Who was that bitch? He was fine as the fuck!"

"Rumi. He damn sure is fine."

"I just know you hopped down."

"No, we were just chatting because I ran into him on accident. I don't have time to be talking with niggas girl."

"It aint never that bad to not have friend. You might have just let your future husband swag off bih." Essynce laughed at her over the top friend as they headed to the register to pay for the few pieces they found. Leaving Forever 21 the girls headed to Macy's, as they shopped around a little boy ran past them

"Scuse me!" He said with a giggle.

"Lyberti, stop running dude!"

That voice caused a chill to run down Essynce back and the hair on the back of her neck stood at attention. She refused to turn around, she couldn't even move if she wanted too.

"My bad."

"Oh, your fine, he is too cute and polite!" Naomi said admiring the little boy who stood there smiling at them. Essynce looked at him confused, he favored Landon, but she never recalled Landon saying he had any kids.

"Don't be fooled, that lil nigga bad as shit."

"He's the cutest and the cute ones usually are." While Naomi was holding conversation Essynce was trying to fade to the back. She didn't want to be seen, so an exit out of the awkward situation was what she needed and quickly.

"Landon can you buy me these? They are on sa—"

Out of all the days and time she just had to be in the damn shoe section in Macy's trapped by her enemies. If it wasn't for bad luck, Essynce swore she wouldn't have any.

"Well, hey Essynce," Leylan said with an ominous look on her face. It was a mix between disgusted and angry.

"Hi, look I don't want any problems. I tried to explain." Leylan cut her off by raising her hand to stop her. Leylan started walking towards her and Essynce didn't know rather to square up or run.

"The funny thing about betrayal, it never comes from your enemies. Watch your back Essynce." Leylan said coldly and low so that only the two of them could hear. She would never create a scene and she didn't have to. From the fear Leylan could smell reeking off of Essynce, she got her message loud and clear.

"Try to have a good day." Leylan walked away heading for the young boy who still had Naomi fascinated. Essynce was in grave danger and Naomi was playing with a baby, not that she could have helped in anyway but still.

"We have to go."

"But I didn't find—"

"I'll be in the car." Essynce cut her off walking away quickly before Landon could get to her. Essynce damn near ran making her way back out to the mall area to find the quickest exit. As she neared the exit she ran right into Rumi.

"Excu—"

"Damn, we got to stop meeting like this. Why you look scared miss? You good?"

"I'm fine, I just have to go" Essynce tried walking around Rumi but he didn't budge, he looked at her with concern

"Whatever your scared of, don't be. I got you ma."

"You don't even know me, and I highly doubt you can help me! Can you move please, I need to get going."

"Let at least make sure you make it to your car, I wouldn't be a man if I didn't at least do that." Rumi threw his hair back and out of his face as he turned and started walking alongside Essynce out the door.

"Ah fuck!"

"What's wrong?"

"I didn't drive, my friend did, and she has the keys. This is exactly why I didn't want to come out. I need to get out of here." Essynce started talking to herself trying plan her next move. She needed to not only get out of the same vicinity of the Miahgo's but the state as well.

"Calm down Essynce, I can take you wherever you need to go. Don't even trip."

"I'm sorry, but I don't even know you like that to be accepting rides from you. No offense"

"Look at me, do I look like a nigga that would do something to you?" Taking a real look at Rumi, Essynce had to admit he could get the business but he had run into her at the wrong point in her life.

Standing at a good six feet four, Rumi was fine from the top of his silky hair to the full lips he possessed that looked like he could make you scream your own name, he had a really light complexion giving away the notion of him being mixed with something. He sported a blinged out grill that made Essynce clamp her legs shut or the flood gates would open. The dark brown eyes he possessed were tricky though, she couldn't read them at all.

Light blue stone wash Embellish jeans and a maroon bomber jacket set his outfit off and if that wasn't enough the way he licked his lips definitely took the cake.

"Looks can be deceiving." Essynce was contemplating taking him up on his offer. She just needed to get out of that mall like yesterday.

"Okay what you want to do, just sit in my car until your homegirl comes out? I'll let you hold my wallet while we wait if that makes you feel better." Essynce laughed as he pats his pockets like he was going to give it to her.

"I'm not scared of you Rumi, I got a kill shot one arm or not. If you're not busy I would like to wait for Naomi, you don't have to take me all the way across town,"

"Follow me kill shot." Rumi lead the way over to his Tahoe as they hopped in, Essynce gave him directions to where they had parked so they could wait for Naomi to come out. Essynce would have text her but of course her phone had bee dead since they arrived at the mall.

"You smoke?"

"No."

"You mind if I do?"

"Its your car. What are you back here for anyway?"

"My nigga from the sandbox called me and needed my help with his business, it wasn't something that could be handled over the phone, so I hopped on a plane and came to help my nigga out. What do you do Essynce?"

"You're a good friend, I'm sure he appreciates that. Can I see your phone?" Essynce had totally dodged his question of her occupation, if she hadn't learned shit else from her experience; She knew niggas weren't too fond of any type of law enforcement.

"Here you go."

"Thank you... Hey I'm sitting out here waiting for you, ok"

Essynce handed Rumi his phone back and the radio took over the awkward silence in the truck.

"Here she comes, thank you I'm sure you are busy with your friend, but I appreciate you looking out."

"Say less ma, it aint shit. I'm a nice dude, but yeah be easy Essynce."

"Bye Rumi."

Dez

"What time should I be expecting you?"

"I aint gone lie to you ma, I don't even know. I'm kind of tied up right now and I don't know how long it's gone take me to wrap this shit up."

"Oh, ok well just let me know if you have time."

"You got that ma." Dez disconnected the call as he threw his phone into his lap, he had been posted outside of this house waiting on the perfect opportunity. Dez was out for two things, blood and his money and not specifically in that order.

Dez loved Emory with everything in him. He carried her the only way he was taught to, it wasn't like he had great examples on how to treat a woman, so he did what he saw. He thought that Emory would forever be there for him rather he was right or wrong, of course like any nigga in the game he did his dirt and did her dirty in the process, but he thought he was taking care of home.

What burned him up about this whole situation was that Emory was so quick to jump ship as soon as she could but here she was down her in Kansas City being a modern-day Bonnie. Where was all that riding shit when he needed her? The ink wasn't even dry on the paperwork before Emory hightailed her ass back down to Kansas City with all his money. True the house was paid for, so he would never be homeless, but in Dez's mind, Emory should have stayed down until the come up.

The best thing the courts ever did was fuck up on Dez's case evidence resulting in his early release. Although he was prepared to sit and do his time after his so called right hand man snitched, getting out early do to the government's fuck up was even better. For the short time that Dez did sit locked up he had time to think about all the dumb shit that lead hi right where he was.

Like any nigga doing time he wanted to make things right with his main lady and get his shit together when time permitted. Emory wasn't answering any of his calls and when he finally got a visit from his mama and found out that Emory had shook the town he was livid. Dez immediately vowed that as soon as he touched down Emory had to pay; in revenue and blood.

He had been keeping a pretty close eye on Emory when he could. It was kind of hard because she was fucking with the head nigga in the town from Dez had heard his family wasn't to be fucked with and they hadn't been. Well up until recently. Dez had even been entertaining with his new little interest he had found at the gym while plotting.

He was there to blow off some steam and saw a bad ass thick one working out not paying a bit of attention. He went ahead and shot his shot and was surprised when he ally ooped. He knew from Malia's demeanor that she was different, he didn't know exactly what she did for a living, but he imagined something super professional just from her dialogue.

A few weeks ago, they came so close to fucking but when Dez peeped how she was acting, he had to put a stop to it and tell her the real. He really wanted to tell her once he got his bread back and killed Emory he would never step foot back in the state of Missouri, but he kept it G rated.

Dez wheels really started turning in his head when he peeped a few pictured she had set up around her living room and saw the nigga that tried to flex on him in the corner store when he first ran down on Emory. He wanted to ask her how she knew dude but didn't want to set off any alarms considering he didn't really divulge what type of business he was intown handling.

But something told him he needed to keep playing Malia close and his gut was right, Malia had lead him right to Emory and didn't even know it.

Sitting outside Dez watched as Emory loaded another bad into her car before she removed a key from her key ring and placed it under a pot on the porch before hopping in her car and leaving. Dez pulled out and remained a good distance behind her so she wouldn't get suspicious. Seeing that they were heading downtown Dez fell back a little bit on the highway but maintained closeness.

Emory pulled into the parking garage of the Marriott Homestead and grabbed a few bags out of the car heading to the front desk to check in is what Dez assumed so he waited. Once Emory walked towards the elevator, Dez gave his keys to the valet and hurried inside.

"Don't fucking scream." Dez rushed into the elevator right before it closed and pushed his hand over Emory's mouth to muffle her sounds.

"Act normal and get to your room, Em don't try me ma, I will snap your fucking neck" Emory nodded her head with tears streaming down her red cheeks. When the two made it inside the suite, Dez looked around.

"You look like you are staying for a minute, that nigga go to jail too?" Dez had to throw his shade. As mad as he was at Emory that didn't take away his attraction to her, she was the baddest bitches he had ever laid eyes on with her exotic features. Her eyes are what attracted him initially and everything else was just a plus to him.

He eyed her puffy red face, her short stature and banging body; he was literally having to think murderous thoughts to keep his dick from rocking up at the moment.

"Sit down, let's talk."

"Dez just take me to the bank, I will give you everything I have. Just leave me be" Emory pleaded.

"I said sit down Em. That always had been a problem of yours; you never could follow directions for shit. I'm gone get my money, no doubt about that, but let's talk."

Emory sat down slowly as far away from Dez as she possibly could, that didn't matter to him he just grabbed the chair and sat it right in front of her, so he could look at her eyes while he said what he had to say.

"I'm going to ask you a few questions, you will answer them honestly. Every lie that spills out your mouth will equal how many days I torture your ass before I kill you. Understand?" Emory nodded her head.

"Use your words ma, I said, do you understand?"

"Yeah!" Emory was scared sad and pissed all rolled into one, if she wasn't in such a hurry to leave Lessiin's place she would have been more observing of her surroundings. If she could somehow get to her phone she knew everything would be ok. But she had to play this game with Dez smartly.

"First question, why were you so quick to run when shit hit the fan?" Dez leaned forward with his elbows on his thighs as he waited for her to answer.

"Honestly Dez, you had me fucked up. Yeah you took care of things financially, but what did I have? You treated me like your child!"

"Yo that's some ungrateful shit. I took care of you, you didn't work, you didn't have to hustle! I did! I was your fucking daddy if you ask me." Dez hated the bullshit Emory was spitting right now.

"You asked, I answered. When you got knocked there was twenty-five thousand in that safe, after I paid off your house because I knew you wouldn't be gone for life, I had to survive!" Emory was crying explaining to him why she did what she did.

"I don't want to hear that shit. Next question, why did you kill my baby?"

"What?"

"You fucking heard me! My momma told me, remember Em if you lie, I torture your ass so just be real ma."

"I didn't kill shit! What type of bitch you take me for?"

"So, you saying my mama lied on you? My mama a damn liar?"

"Your bald head ass mama is a lot more than a liar, but we won't go there right now. Nigga I was never pregnant. The day you got sentenced, your side piece Joya let it be known that I better be ready to play step mommy to y'all baby. I shook about a few weeks right after."

"Joya?"

"Yeah nigga the little red project bitch you slid up in every chance you got! Remember now?"

"Chill out man, where the baby at then? Nobody told me shit."

"That's between you, Joya and God himself. But your funky ass mama knew, because she was surely happy about 'finally' being a granny." Emory used air quotes and her attitude was on a smooth one hundred as she recalled the day.

"Ok, I got that. Last question, where is my bread? I know you paid off the house, but that still left you with a grip."

"Asshole that was damn near five years ago, the fuck you think I eat air? But I can pay you that shit, take me to the bank first thing in the morning nigga. I can't believe your ass is crossing city limits trying to kill me over a few stacks Dez!"

"It's the principle! You don't get a nigga back like that Emory! I know I did some ill shit, I know I wasn't the best nigga, but we were young. You didn't give a nigga a chance. To right his wrongs, you shook the spot and didn't give a fuck. When your folks weren't there, I was."

"Dez we leaned on each other, please stop making it seem like I was a damsel in distress or a charity case. My nigga who helped you with your first pack? Huh? Me, that's who! When you were short cause you were trickin' off your shit in the club or your 'workers' were fucking you over, who made moves took out loans or what the fuck ever to help 'us'? Me, that's who!"

"So why did you leave!?" Dez screamed

"Because it wasn't shit to stay for!"

The two of them had both stood up huffing and puffing as they finally expressed their feelings. While tears streamed down Emory's face and Dez nostrils flared suddenly their lips came close and a passionate kiss commenced.

The two kissed like long lost lovers in the middle of the suite. Dez grabbed the back of Emory's neck as he tongued her down. Emory had closed her eyes and grabbed the front of Dez shirt balling it up in her small hands. Suddenly Dez pulled away and looked Emory dead in her eyes with confusion and lust. Emory's expression mirrored his.

Nothing could be heard but heavy breathing as Dez picked Emory up carrying her over to the couch and roughly tossing her down. Emory pulled her hoodie over head as Dez started attacking her nipples. Dez had dropped his pants in the process and the two of them roamed their hand all over the other.

Unexpectedly, both of their cell phones sounded off at the same time stopping them in the middle of their steamy session. As if realization sat in, the both of them separated and moved away from the other.

"You always could fuck a niggas head up." Dez shook his head imagining just how far things could have gone had the phones not stopped them. Dez walked over to his jacket and pulled his phone out of his pocket to see who had called. Seeing it was Malia had caused Dez to get a funny feeling in his stomach, he was feeling a bit of guilt.

Since meeting Malia and chilling with her he had formed a different way of thinking. Malia had qualities that rubbed off on Dez, he was trying to get himself together. Texting Malia back he turned and looked at Emory sitting on the couch looking sad.

"You love him?"

"Huh, what?"

"You heard me the first time Em, you love cuz?"

"Yeah, but that shit dead."

"Why every time shit gets ruff your first instinct is to run? You got to stop that shit girl."

"Look at you trying to school the kid. Don't matter anyway; you are killing me after you get paid anyway." Emory rolled her eyes thinking she would probably be better off dead anyway.

"Aint nobody killing your wanna be tuff ass. But I had to get you to have this conversation with me ma. That shit was burning a nigga up thinking you shook and killed his seed. Then when I saw you with little homie at the Wal-Mart, I just snapped"

"I didn't know you thought that this whole time Dez, I swear on my life I would have never done no shit like that."

"I believe you kid. Look, I aint tripping over that bread either. You just got to do one thing though."

"What nigga?" Emory crossed her arms thinking he was about to be on some other shit

"You got to go back and make shit work with dude. Whatever you mad about, talk about it and rock with it."

"Why you care Dez?"

"Because I been doing my research, and I hear dude is solid as they come, the type of nigga you need in your life ma."

"I love you too Dez." Emory joked rolling her eyes

"Yeah love deez. Oh, another thing, keep your ass off them poles man!"

"Fuck you! You owe down nigga, gone push me and knock me the fuck out in the middle of Wal-Mart."

"That's my bad ma." Dez through his hands up trying not to let his laugh seep out that he was holding in.

"Get out! You make me sick, when you going back to the Lou since you done stalking me now?"

"Shit I don't even know. I met me a little situation and KC ain't as bad as I thought it would be. I might post up for real." Dez walked back over to his jacket throwing it on.

"I'm gone walk down with you; I need to get something out my car."

As the two held conversation, Emory couldn't help but feel like a weight had just been lifted off her shoulder. As they made it to the lobby laughing and joking an angry voice came from behind her that made her knees buckle.

"Aw yeah, that how we rockin huh?"

"Lessiin, it's not what it looks like"

"Really Dez, this the business you had to take care of?" Malia screeched standing next to Lessiin in the hotel Lobby.

Loyal

"Why are we here bruh?" Rumi was sleepy and ready to help Loyal with he had going on, so he could get back to California. He hated coming to Kansas City for long periods of time. Something about the city just brought him down. Maybe it was the memories or maybe it was just the aura he got, but either way he was ready to head back west. Kansas City would forever be home, but he had outgrown it.

"Nigga, I haven't talked to my Big Mama. After I check on her then we can go do that."

"I ain't know Big Mama moved over here shit." Rumi followed Loyal in the house, when they got inside the house it was quiet. Normally the TV would be on at least and that alone was a red flag to Loyal.

"Make sure she didn't fall or nothing down here, I'm gone check upstairs." Loyal ran upstairs in search of Big Mama. He checked all the bedrooms and didn't see her or anything suspicious. Going back downstairs he met Rumi in the kitchen. Big mama never left the house so Loyal was worried.

As Loyal went through his phone to find the nurse that looked after Big Mama they heard some noise at the front door. Rumi tapped Loyal telling him to be quiet and pulled out his gun standing at an angle that gave him the perfect view and shot of the front door.

"Mama!!" Dimengo yelled coming through the front door

"She ain't here."

"Where she at?"

"That's what I'm trying to figure out. When the last time you came by here?"

"Shit, been a minute. I just came to get my mail." Dimengo shrugged jogging up the stairs to grab his mail.

"Damn ya pops ain't bout shit." Rumi said with a mug on his face. When Dimengo came back down he looked Rumi up and down before looking at Loyal and heading out. Rumi stood firm in the doorway not moving an inch to allow Dimengo through. Like the coward he was he turned his body side ways to avoid bumping Rumi on his way out the kitchen.

"You ain't gone look for Big Mama?" Loyal asked already knowing the answer.

"Aint that what you doing? What you want me to do?"

"You a sucka ass nigga bruh" Loyal spat as Dimengo turned and walked out the house without a care in the world.

"Aye he dropped something."

"Fuck that nigga."

"Nah bro, this looks like a check." Rumi handed Loyal the envelope and he pulled it out. Sure, enough it was a check for a beneficiary.

"Who the fuck made him a beneficiary and for what?" Loyal said to himself.

"I can find out soon as I get to my laptop." Rumi folded the check up and placed it in his pocket."

"Let me call this nurse."

"Hello Mr., Loyal, does Big Mama need me today?"

"Well that's why I'm calling, she isn't here, and I thought you would know where she would be."

"Really? No, her son and his wife called me about two weeks ago saying they were taking Big Mama out of town for a family vacation and my services wouldn't be needed."

"They said what?! Big Mama wouldn't go nowhere with that base head."

"I'm so sorry Mr. Loyal, I thought you knew, oh my God." Tiana said nervously, she had been assisting Big Mama for quite some time and she loved her like she was her family.

"I'll call you back Tiana." Loyal disconnected the call and his whole body was on fire. Loyal had a feeling in the pit of stomach that something bad had happened to his grandmother and he was willing to bet his life that Dimengo scumbag ass had hands all in it.

"Let's go!" Loyal took off out the house jogging to his car. Rumi was right behind him ready to ride for whatever. Big Mama was like his second mother when they were growing up so there's no doubt that he would kill Dimengo himself if he had done anything to her.

"Aye Landon bro, its time! You know what's up; I'll be there in twenty minutes!" Loyal said throwing the phone in his lap as he weaved in and out of traffic. His blood was boiling, and he could only imagine what Dimengo had done to his own mother. Just the thought of Big Mama taking her last breath had Loyal's heart about to burst through his chest.

"She alright bro. I swear she is." Rumi tried reassuring him but deep in Loyal's heart he knew the opposite. He had a dream earlier that week that he was at funeral, but he never got to the point in the dream where he saw whose it was. He felt like that was Big Mama coming to him in his dreams.

"You can't look that shit up on your phone?" Loyal asked.

"I wasn't trying to, but I'm already on it." Loyal looked over and sure enough Rumi already had his phone out going to town on the screen. His boy was as loyal as they got, that's one thing he never had to question.

Pulling into the warehouse, Loyal saw three cars already there, so he parked and hopped out. Putting in the code that Lessiin had given him granted him access inside as Rumi trailed behind him.

"What's up?" Lessiin greeted his brother.

"Who's the white boy?" Landon asked seriously.

"Who's white?"

"You Paul Wall," Landon didn't care who you were, you were catching these jokes.

"Chill, that's my other brother Rumi. Rumi, these are my brothers and sister the trips I told you about. That one is Lessiin. The comedian is Landon. And duh, that's Leylan." Loyal introduced.

"You here so that means Loyal trusts you with his life." Lessiin said and turned back to the computer screen. The tension in the air was kind of thick as everyone was in their own respective spaces, but regardless to how they felt about each other at the moment; if one of them needed something, they all came together.

"So, check this out, I hadn't been by Big Mama's in a minute, normally she calls me at least once a week, none of that. We go over there cause I'm thinking she must be mad at the kid or something and Rumi wanted to see her anyway. We get there and it quiet and dark, Big Mama keep that tv going no matter what, so that was red flag. We search the whole crib and Big Mama aint in there at all.

Right before I'm about to call the nurse that's looks after her, Dimengo walks in chumping me off about her, he just worried about his mail. Okay wrapping this story up, he dropped a check rushing to get out. Rumi checking the source now. And the nurse said that about two weeks ago Laila and Dimengo told her she wasn't needed because they were taking her on a family vacation."

"Vacation?" Lessiin sat up looking confused

"This check is registered back to American Life Insurance." Rumi said as he hung up his phone stomping on it and discarding it.

"What's dude deal?" Landon asked lowly as he watched Rumi destroying his own phone

"I don't track shit on my personal phone and if I do that bitch is dead exactly after."

"Makes sense" Leylan cut in looking at Loyal as his chest moved up and down

Loyal looked at Rumi for reassurance before he coolly got up and walked out the room to get himself together. He wouldn't dare cry in a room full of niggas, family or not. Dimengo was sick as fuck, he had done the unimaginable and Loyal was seeing red. Cleaning his face he got his look together trying not to look how he felt. Jersey was going to be fucked up behind this and Loyal knew he was going to have to be her backbone. Making his way back into the area everybody was waiting for him in, Lessiin was surprisingly the first one to stand up and walk over to Loyal.

"Miahgo's stick together no matter what. Remember that when you start feeling like you are all alone." Lessiin had embraced him and spoke into his ear so that only the two of them could hear. Loyal embraced his big brother back and acknowledging what he said.

"I love you too big bro." Loyal patted Lessiin's back as they separated

"Baby boy, you gone be alright my nigga. On God you gone be good, remember that." Landon assured

Leylan walked over giving Loyal a hug and rubbing his back. She stepped back and cleared her throat before she got into savage mode.

"I have the coordinates on Laila and Dimengo's moves from the last two weeks. They must live at this address, cause the coordinates ping back to this location the most daily. Y'all ready?" Leylan was dressed in all black with all her hair pulled into a tight bun. She was ready to put in work on her absentee parents and end some of their troubles. Leylan prayed that Loyal's grandmother was ok, but really, they all knew what that check was about.

"You don't have to go if you don't want to bro." Landon assured knowing that his brother wasn't a killer and he didn't have to be.

"I'm going." Loyal said with assertiveness as everybody looked at him in admiration.

"A savage is being born." Leylan said like a proud parent as she watched Loyal's eyes start to change like the rest of theirs did when they were about to put in work.

"Let's go." Lessiin turned walking to the entrance of the warehouse. When the doors opened, everyone pulled their guns with the exception of Loyal who wasn't packing. Looking like they had seen a ghost everybody stood in shock.

"PopPop!?" Leylan yelled running towards for her grandfather, they hadn't seen him in months and they all knew what he was up to, but they had never gone that long without him.

"Old timer, where the hell you been?!" Landon joked as he slapped hands with Cesare.

"I got your old man lil nigga. Good to see you back amongst the healthy."

"You know they can't keep a real one down PopPop."

"Don't I know it. Who are our guests?"

"This is your grandson Loyal. And the white dude is his brother from another mother." Landon had to do the introductions.

"I'm not white nigga." Rumi laughed.

"Grandson? Who your mama?"

"My mama is Ella Mae Barnes, but the donor that pushed me out is Laila Miahgo." Loyal said with confidence.

"Say word?" Cesare stared at Loyal knowing he was indeed a Miahgo, he favored the triplets in different ways, but his aura screamed the resemblance.

"Word. What can I call you?"

"These three headaches call me PopPop, but my name is Cesare. You let me know what you comfortable with, but make sure you put some respect on that shit youngin." Loyal laughed and nodded his head giving PopPop a handshake and a manly hug.

"You said Ellamae Barnes, huh? That's Dimengo's moms aint it?"

"Yes sir."

"How she doing? I ain't seen Ella in bout twenty years, I didn't know she was holding one of my grandkids over there. Laila ain't gone worry me, shit"

"PopPop, we on our way to a mission. We can catch you up on the way cause you gone need to hear this." Leylan said with a sad look on her face. She knew it wasn't going to be easy to tell PopPop that they were on their way to kill his only daughter but today was the day.

Different thoughts were running through everybody's head as they headed to the other side of town to the house that they knew Dimengo and Laila resided. Leylan could care less about putting her so called parents in the dirt, in her mind it was two less worthless people roaming the earth.

Lessiin had a million different things floating through his mind. He needed to get his personal life in order, but this took priority over that right now. For the first time he was contemplating this being his final assignment. Lyberti came through like a category five hurricane changing his outlook on life for the better. Emory had changed his outlook on love completely. For now, his focus was laying Dimengo out.

Landon didn't care either way the wind blew at this point. He just wanted to get back to how he was before the accident and get back to chasing the bag. Taliyah and Essynce had to be dealt with personally and after he handled that, he was going to put more into his car business hanging up his racing days for good.

Loyal was fucked up, his leading lady wasn't going to be on the sidelines cheering him on. His home was good, he and Jersey were right where they needed to be, but shit would never be the same without Big Mama. He had made up in his mind that tonight, Dimengo would die by his

hands and his hands only.

Laila

"Dimengo, something doesn't feel right."

"You just need some candy, that's all. Don't start that paranoid and superstitious shit right now Lai." Dimengo felt it too, but he would never admit he was scared. He had just gone back to his mother's home and ransacked it looking for the check he knew he had picked up earlier. If it wasn't for his nosey ass son, none of this shit would be happening. He hadn't been by there in weeks, but today of all days when the check was there, he had his want to be tuff ass there looking for his Big Mama.

"But what are we going to do now? The only reason we did that shit was for the payout and now we don't even have that." Laila wasn't a dummy, she knew their days were numbered, she never wanted to bring any harm to Ms. Ella but Dimengo had a way of making her do any and everything she never wanted to do.

As Dimengo paced back and forth in the middle of the damn near empty living room, he was in deep thought. He knew his next move had to be his best move because time was ticking. Thinking about the folder he had, he ran to the bedroom in the back of the town house. He racked through all the clothes that were scattered about looking for that folder. This was his last hope, if this shit didn't pan out, him and Laila might as well skip town and get it the old school pimp way.

Suddenly without warning the power went out.

"Aye was the light bill past due?"

Silence

"Lai! Laila your scary ass hear me talking to you?! Did you pay them people, what the fuck is up with the lights?" Dimengo felt around as he made his way down the short hallway looking for Laila.

"Where the fuck she go?" Dimengo had to check himself, was he that high?

"Lai—what the fuck?" Dimengo yelled as he hit the floor hard. All the street lights in their grimy subdivision had been long gone so it was pitch black in the house. Wanting to kick his own ass for not having his phone to use for light, Dimengo tried to stand up.

"Argh!" he felt the hard hit knock him back down.

"Who the fuck is in my house?! Fight me like a man pussy!" Swiftly the lights cut back on and as soon as Dimengo's vision cleared, he wished he was anywhere else, but right here right now.

Sitting in his home were all four of his children. They were all dressed in black and had the image of animals plastered on their faces.

"Aright, aright y'all got me. Now what, y'all gone kill me? Go ahead muthafuckas! I don't like none of you bastards any fucking way!" Dimengo had made up in his mind he would be dying tonight, so he damn sure wasn't going out like a bitch. If he was going to be taken out by his own kids, he wasn't going to beg them.

Loyal was the first to move in towards Dimengo, he stood over him not saying a word.

"What's this shit? Your initiation or something? You Brandy nigga, trying to be down! You could never be them, they are bred for this shit, you just they little brother. You the one supposed to kill me?" Dimengo taunted Loyal as he stood there soaking in all his words. He laughed a hardy laugh from his soul and Loyal stood there unfazed.

"Where Big Mama at pussy nigga? I ain't never been a bitch, I don't have to pretend to be shit. Nigga, I'm Loyal Miahgo! That's why you spent your whole life trying to tear a bitch down. You're a coward and a bum. Fuck the little yellow school bus my nigga the struggle bus has your picture plastered on the side of that bitch. You wanted to be a Miahgo so bad, but just couldn't make the cut. Fuck you." Loyal never raised his voice or moved a muscle while he spoke with venom dripping from every word. His words alone felt like twenty daggers in Dimengo's head.

Lessiin, Landon and Leylan all stepped up next to him looking at Dimengo on the floor.

"You're right where you're supposed to be, bitch nigga. Beneath us." Leylan spat with a wicked smile.

"Where's Laila, she should have aborted all you pussies like I told her dumb ass too! Four ungrateful bastard ass kids are who I'm leaving behind in my honor. Fucked up." Dimengo wasn't letting up, he knew he wouldn't be making it to see another day, so he was going to go out like the fuck nigga he was.

"Your honor? Nigga you can't sit with us, we don't claim you. You such a bitch nigga we don't even carry your last name fam." Landon spat, felling like he needed to clear that up quickly.

"Don't matter, you bitches still came from my nut sack! Ahhh fuck!"

"You the only bitch in here nigga." Leylan delivered a vicious kick to the middle of Dimengo head cause a wound to open and pour blood down his face.

Lessiin had yet to say a word, which was normal. He felt someone looking at him, so he followed the gaze and made eye contact with Loyal. He could see the yearning for blood in his little brother's eyes. Walking over to him he tapped his arm motioning for him to come to the side and talk to him. While they walked away, Landon and Leylan took turns kicking Dimengo's ass for sport.

"What you feeling bro? I know that look, you looked just like me when I was about to act out the very first time. I ain't gone lie to you, at first you gone feel like you lifted a ton of weight of your shoulders. But them dreams come and that inner voice start talking shit, if you can't handle that shit don't fuck wit it. But if you need it, like I think you do, well you know."

Loyal stared at Lessiin for what felt like an eternity, he was having an inner battle with himself. He had a thirst for blood but then he had an angel way in the back telling him to walk away. Out of nowhere Loyal produced a hunting knife and turned quickly walking over to Dimengo who looked like Martin from that boxing episode.

Walking up swiftly, he grabbed Dimengo by his hair that had been slicked back at one point. He held his head back and took the slicing him from left to right damn near decapitating him. Loyal stared Dimengo in his eyes the entire time, even after his eyes had rolled in the back of his head Loyal remained in the same position.

Lessiin walked over slowly not to shock him out of his trance while he still had that knife in his hand and that look in his eyes.

"This pussy still smiling." Loyal said as one lone tear fell from his right eye.

"Aye you just like Fat Ma with that knife shit. Let him go Loyal" Landon coached.

"You okay?" Leylan asked knowing how it felt after that first kill, that's the one that stuck with you for the rest of your life. The others you would remember, but that first one held a special place.

Throwing Dimengo's lifeless body down, he landed in a twisted position cause his head to do a complete three sixty.

"You couldn't shoot that nigga." Landon asked turning his head at the site before him. Landon was never into the torture technique like his siblings, he was a shot to the middle of the eyes type and get it over with. Loyal dropped the knife but never took his eyes off Dimengo. He didn't feel anything, no relief, no sadness, just nothing.

Lessiin inched closer pulling his brother into his arms, he held him as Landon and Leylan came over and joined the group hug.

"I knew something was wrong with y'all ass who the fuck group hugs in the middle of a damn crime scene!" Rocky spat as he entered the house dressed identical to the rest. Not far behind him was Seneca.

"Really Leylan, looks like you had a good time."

"That wasn't my work that was baby bro" Leylan said like she was a proud mama.

"What? No, Loyal baby are you okay?" Seneca asked concerned

"Yes ma'am." Loyal replied still in a zoned out state.

"He gone be straight." Lessiin interrupted "Where PopPop go?"

"Y'all need to come next door, quickly!" Seneca said turning to leave out the same way they came.

Everybody filed out and headed next door to see what was going on. Loyal was the last one to come in and when he did he broke down. He cried like he had never cried before at what he saw. There wasn't one dry eye in that raggedy townhouse. Everybody had tears flowing, even Lessiin.

"Come here baby boy."

"Give me a minute." Loyal got off the floor and rushed out the house, when he made it outside he fell to his knees again, this time he was praying. He was thanking God for everything he could and asking for forgiveness. Standing up he saw his siblings right there with their heads bowed. He really knew at that moment that they really did have each other's backs for life.

Walking back in the house he rushed up to Big Mama not wanting to hurt her, but he needed to hug her, so he knew this was real.

"I know you didn't think you were gone get rid of an old lady that fast did you LoLo?"

"LoLo?!" Everyone said in unison and laughed at Loyal's facial expression.

"Chill, only Jersey and Big Mama call me that shi-stuff"

"Big mama, tell us what happened." Rocky asked as everyone tuned in listening to the story. To know that Dimengo would do his own mama grimy was all Loyal needed to hear to not feel a twinge of guilt. He was honored to have ridded the world of one less fuck nigga.

Cesare

Looking at his one and only child Cesare couldn't really pinpoint one emotion he felt when it came his child. Like any parent, you want to love and protect your child, but Cesare was torn between torturing and ending her life quickly.

"Just kill me already daddy, I been dead for years anyway." Laila said in a pitiful tone.

"Laila, you could have been anything in this world. There was nothing you couldn't have and or do. You had the brains, the beauty, the full package. But you chose to follow a bum. Did you ever think about why Dimengo approached you all those years ago?"

Laila lifted her head looking confused.

"Dimengo has always been a scumbag, his inherited it from his own bitch as daddy. His pops was a so-called pimp back in the day. Well he tried to teach his son the game, but that shit was an epic fail. Dimengo was born a fuckup, it's in his DNA. That pimp shit didn't work well for him, especially when the OG of the strip he was trying to trick on cut him off. He wasn't having that shit and Dimengo knew it. So, like the bitch that he is he went running to his daddy about his problems and his pops tried to press that OG. Long story short OG hired somebody to take care of Dimengo's pops and that somebody was me."

When the realization of what Cesare was saying sat in, Laila's body rocked as she let out a gut-wrenching scream. Her entire miserable life was flashing like a slide show in her head. She had been bamboozled her entire life. Nothing was real, and Laila had failed. She turned her back on her father and her children for a nigga who was hell bent on getting get back at her father. He used abused and spit Laila out.

The thoughts were too much for her to handle, Laila wanted to get high right then and there. She didn't want to live, she didn't care if Cesare filled her body with a million bullets at this point. As if Cesare had read her mind, he laid a gun and a pack of pure raw uncut white girl on the table. Laila's eyes lit up like a Christmas tree.

"So Dimengo isn't here now Laila, you have to make a decision on your own. You have two options, so listen and listen carefully. You can pick drugs like I see you are salivating over, or you can take this gun and go kill Dimengo and get your life together. If you choose the first option, know that we will never have anything to do with you, you are dead to us.

Laila sat there contemplating. She had been damn near alone her whole life anyway. What was the point in trying to straighten up? She saw the way her kids looked at her; there was no repairing those feelings. It wasn't like they were babies, they were adults and had their minds made up.

She thought about exactly how good she would feel once she got her hands on that pack. She knew if she didn't have shit else in this world, she would be just fine getting high. She shook as she walked forward to make her decision. Her hands were trembling and the flashes from the past still kept flashing in her mind as she took what felt like the walk of death.

Making it to the table, Laila picked up the gun and turned around. Cesare smiled like a proud father happy that Laila had made the right decision. As she slowly walked to the door she turned around looking at Cesare.

"I love you daddy. I love all of my children. I love Seneca for taking the triplets in and I love Ellamae for taking in Loyal." Laila raised the gun.

"Noooo!!"

Bang

Laila had placed the gun in her mouth and pulled the trigger. She had chosen a different option.

Malia Rose

"Your Honor, the state has no substantial evidence against my clients, we move for all charges except the possession be dismissed." Finelley concluded before taking a seat.

"Prosecution?"

"Your Honor, the state does not object."

"Jream Sirtan and Lessiin Miahgo, the state of Missouri has dismissed the first-degree murder charge. However, we find you both guilty on count two of possession of marijuana over the legal limit of 0.5." The judge went on to explain how they would be sentenced to probation for eighteen months and the rules regarding that.

After court Malia headed to her office and got a huge shock, sitting in her chair was Dez.

"What are you doing here?"

"Waiting for you, let's talk."

"I'm working."

"Correction, you were working. Now that court is out you have time and no you don't have any appointments for the rest of the afternoon. Sit down ma." Dez wasn't about to play with Malia's spoiled ass. She got mad and ran out the hotel before she heard the full story and had been dodging Dez for over a week. Although Dez caught a mean two piece from Lessiin, him and Emory were at least able to talk to dude and get an understanding of the whole situation.

Dez had apologized and Emory had taken heed to his conditions of letting her live and worked shit out with her man. Now, Dez had to get the stubborn State Prosecutor to follow suit.

"So, what you saw wasn't quite what it seemed. Yes, Emory and I had history and I was still caught up on some things that transpired regarding our split. Honestly, I was only here in the town to kill her ass. I wanted to teach her a lesson for how she played me. But in the midst of that, I met this woman, she had me thinking of other ways to channel my aggression towards the situation, she made me realize that it was time to move on and go with the flow of the future."

"Who is the woman?" Malia teased, she had already talked to Emory and Lessiin and knew what was up, but she had to make Dez sweat. She was a little upset that he was there trying to kill somebody but all in her house, but who was she kidding her family was the underworld savages.

"Stop playing ma, you got a nigga switching area codes and changing my life. You got to work with a nigga though. Plus, you the Feds so this gone take a minute for me to get used to and shit." Dez laughed as Malia playfully punched his arm. He sat on her desk and pulled her close.

"You know what they say about good girls going bad."

"But that's the thing, I'm a bad girl gone good." Malia kissed Dez passionately, as their tongues intertwined and Dez trailed his hands up her skirt palming her thick back side.

"Aye I will fuck the shit out of you in here." Dez said looking at Malia as she bit her bottom lip.

"I mean the door is locked." She winked

"Bad girl gone good my ass! Come on, I already told that fruit at the front you was leaving after court."

"Thomas is not a fruit."

"Yeah and I'm a saint, anyway let's go Attorney Rose." Dez kissed Malia on her forehead and stood up helping her pull her skirt back over her wide hips.

"We gone have to do something about these suites ma, niggas committing crimes on purpose in Kansas City just to get tried by your fine ass." Malia and Dez laughed as they left her office building hand in hand.

Epilogue

Two years later...

"Dude, you eating again? I swear you gone look like a foreign Oompa Loompa you keep eating like that." Landon said as he teased Emory

"When are you going home? Why you worried about what I'm gone look like anyway?" Emory was snappy and uncomfortable already and Landon's jokes just weren't going to fly today.

"Leave her alone!"

"Oh, shit it's an attack of the preggo zombies!" Landon ducked and ran through the house knowing he wasn't being chased, but Jersey had dope ass aim and almost everything she threw hit its target.

"They gone fuck you up." Loyal laughed passing the blunt to Landon.

"I'm already knowing. What's wrong with you?" Lessiin had a serious look on his face as he faced a personal blunt like he was stressed.

"Yeah, tell em what's wrong." Jream teased, he already knew what had Lessiin in such a frenzy and he found it funny as hell.

"I'm about to fuck my life up."

"Huh?"

"Tell em nigga, tell em why you scared." Jream egged on

"Shut up Nightmare, nigga can't think. I shouldn't have never told yo ass shit. Anyway, I'm about to ask Emory to marry a nigga." Lessiin took a deep pull from his blunt.

Suddenly all the guys busted out laughing, Rocky laughing the hardest.

"It aint that bad youngin. I swear to you, it's the best feeling in the world knowing you found your match, knowing that you got something that nobody else has. You come home to some shit that was designed just for you. Boy you gone make me take Sen up out of here." Rocky passed the blunt to Jream who just nodded his head like he was married already.

"Fuck you shaking your head for like y'all married already."

"Well."

"Well what?!" Loyal, Landon and Lessiin said in unison.

"Y'all remember when I took Leylan to Vegas for her graduation gift?"

"How could we forget, her spoiled ass talked about her 'gradcation" so much I was ready to throw her on my back and walk her chubby ass there." Landon fussed.

"Chill on my *wife* nigga."

"Wife?! Y'all eloped down there?!" Loyal asked shocked they had kept it a secret that long.

"Yep."

"Oh my God!!" they heard a scream and took off in the house for the women

"What happened?!" Lessiin yelled thinking Jersey or Emory had gone into labor.

"Leylan got married bae!" All the girls were hugging and smiling so excited.

"We just found out. I'm fucking you up Nightmare! Why you didn't give my sister a wedding?"

"She didn't want one dude, I tried to talk her out of it."

"No really y'all, I just wanted that intimacy and life event to be shared with the love of my life in privacy. I'm sorry, I didn't tell anybody until now, but I would do it all again." Leylan had brought all the girls to tears and the men were very proud of their baby girl. It took a while for them to get over the fact that she had been stripping, but they got over it and moved on. It took Lessiin a little longer than everybody else, but he came around.

"Damn, y'all niggas trippin, I'm still tryna set a world record" Landon said plopping on the couch.

"What record? Jersey asked confused.

"Fuckin bitches, duh sis" Landon held his hand out as if that was the dumbest question in the world.

"Your dick gone fall off." Emory through a pillow, hitting Landon right in the face.

"Damn you and Jersey been practicing catch and shit at them yoga classes?" Everybody erupted in laughter. Lessiin took that as his cue to do what he had to do. He moved over slowly towards Emory and stood in front of her.

"What's wrong bae? You okay?"

"Where is Lyberti?"

"He went to go get my phone out the kitchen, but his little ass probably in there eating again."

"So, look," Lessiin kneeled down in front of Emory and she looked confused as everybody else except the guys.

"When I met you, we had this weird ass connection. I mean it was a shock I didn't shoot yo ass for kissing me. But anyway, it was fate that brought us back together that day in the corner store because I never go in there. The way you clung to my son and took him as your own sealed the deal for a nigga, you were down from day one no questions asked, and a nigga could never ask for more. You give when you don't have, you're the most selfless woman I have ever come in contact with. Your mouth makes me want to play in rush hour traffic sometimes, but then I might miss ya ass, so I stay. Any day now you are bringing my baby into the world, but after that a nigga just want to know if you'll be my wife?" Lessiin held his breath as he watched Emory stare at him for what felt like forever, but was probably only seconds.

"I Wouldn't want any other title in the world, then your wife bae. YES!!!" The two kissed each other as if they would never see each other again, when they separated everybody started giving there congrats and praise.

"Yessss!!!" the girls rushed Emory

"That was the hoodest, most heartfelt proposal I have ever seen." Leylan joked.

"It was the Lessiin way." PopPop added proud of all his grandchildren.

The triplets and Loyal had gone out to the den area so they could talk.

"Yo this shit is mad real, I love y'all." Loyal said to his siblings.

"I love y'all too. We ain't just three the hard way no more, but we still the muthafuckin Miahgo's." Landon boasted.

"Family full of savages. I wouldn't want to be related to anybody else. Muthafuckas might not understand us and that's okay. Our Savage Aint For Everybody, but they gotta respect something!" Lessiin said as he raised his glass and his siblings did the same.

"Loyal! Hurry up, Jersey's water just broke!" Emory yelled outside.

"Aw shit another Miahgo is on the way!" Landon was hype as everybody piled out the house headed to the hospital to welcome their new baby girl.

The End

Sneak Peek

Coming Soon

Husler's Mentality

They Meet

The music was loud and jumping, everyone in attendance was either drunk or high but the club was lit. Not the normal function I usually come to, but I was definitely here for the vibe. With my big brother and good friend by my side, I was vibing. As we made our way from the extremely long bar line we finally found a clear spot to post up. As Juicy J let everyone in the club know that Bandz Will Make Her Dance, there was a slight disturbance coming from the doorway. As a crew about six deep made their way inside, you could tell they had to be of some importance or very popular, either way their presence was felt.

The whole crew gave off the aura of dominance and money, all different shades, styles, statures but they were a unit. As they came in, different ones getting stopped by various people in their path, I kept right on dancing in my spot and having a good time with my people. A few of them looked familiar but the town wasn't as big as people thought and in my line of work, it was possible I had seen them around. As Mac Dre started blasting through the speakers the club turned up quick. I pulled my phone out recording my very animated brother 'thizz dancing' to the beat. As I finished up my laughter and recording I felt a pair of strong arms wrap around my waist alarming me.

Very much a not so single woman, I didn't know who was this bold to have me wrapped up in the middle of the dance floor and as soon as I turned around with attitude on ten ready to light off in their ass, I paused. I was stuck you could say, standing behind me a little short due to my five-inch heels I sported stood the finest nigga I had ever laid eyes on. Eyes real low from intoxication, I could smell the loud weed through his clothes, but it wasn't overbearing, just there. Light kissed by the sun skin, nice medium sized kissable lips, his low-cut Cesar was so on point I got sea sick staring at his waves too long and a small neatly trimmed goatee. Homeboy was fine, period. His whole presence screamed "RUN NOW" and if the tattoos that decorated his entire body that was exposed didn't scare me off, the tattoo going right across his eyebrow definitely gave me

"Do you always hold woman up in the club that you don't know?" I asked him talking into his ear due to all the noise around us.

"Maybe. Aint like I'm a stranger, shit you already know my government name and I don't even know yours." He spoke back smoothly in my ear never lightening up the hold he had on my waist.

"Aye nigga, get yo ass off my little sister!" I heard my brother fuss, but not his normal mean voice. This tone was a joking one, which actually surprised me.

"Aw, nigga this me!" Sexy said back taking one of arms from around me and leaving the other to shake hands with my brother.

"Where the fuck you been at?" My brother asked taking a sip of his drink and acknowledging some of the other guys who had gathered around us. They all shook hands and I also offered a few smiles to the ones I knew from around. Like the niggas I knew them to be they wanted to know about my friend Aleesia who stood their awkwardly. She wasn't the clubbing type at all, but we had dragged her out with us and you could tell.

Very pleasant to the eyes, Aleesia was mixed with Jamaican and black, she stood at five foot five inches tall with the body of a video vixen. She had light brown eyes giving her look an even more exotic feel. You would think she would be the most conceited female this side of the Midwest, but she was quite the opposite. Baby girl was quiet and shy, we worked together for a year and it took six months for her to even hold a full conversation.

"I been low key my nigga, just trying to stay out the way." Sexy said holding conversation with my brother.

"How y'all know each other NiNi?" my brother asked looking at me like I was keeping a secret or some shit.

"He's a regular irritation." I replied smartly making him hold his unoccupied hand to his chest in fake hurt.

"Aw yeah? That's how we rockin ma, I'm hurt?" He joked

"I call a spade a spade. Nice fit tho" I said taking a sip of my Blue Muthafucka.

"I'm calling corporate on your ass, on Monday!" He said smiling showing his perfect set of thirty-two white teeth.

"Snitch." I playfully rolled my eyes.

"What's up lil one, you look different outside the store." He spoke to Aleesia who smiled and looked away in true shy girl fashion.

"So how do you know my brother?" I asked him turning around to face him, he tightened his grip making me move even closer to him.

"Been knowing Nas since he was jit. Don't remember ever seeing you though, and I remember everything." He said smartly biting on his bottom lip making the seat of my leggings moist.

"Well umm I don't know what to say about that. I wasn't an in the mix type sister so that's probably how you missed me." I said trying to sound confident.

"Yeah, sounds about right. Here." He said pulling a flip phone out of his jean pocket and motioning it towards me, my nose instantly turned up and not for the reason you think.

"You got me fucked up if you think my number is going in your trap phone." I spat moving out of grasp and a crooked smile etched across his face.

"Pipe down lil mama, my other phone is dead. I wasn't even trying to play you like that, but I like how you peeped game real quick." He said invading her space once again, "Now put your number in here and I lose that attitude, ain't nobody fazed by that little shit."

Rolling my eyes, I grabbed the damn flip phone and put my number in it handing it back to him, so he could do the rest. I hardly remembered how to work that shit so that was his problem now.

"Aight, I'm about to go kick it with my niggas. Don't get this club cleared out, I see everything." He said in a demanding tone

"Akeo, you are not my nigga. You don't have to watch me baby, I'm a big girl." I said twirling in small circle around him and running my hands down his chest.

"Yeah, you are a big girl, so you should know the price to pay when fucking with a real nigga. You can play all you want to but know that those pretty little hands will have their blood on them" was all Akeo said before he nodded his head at my brother before walking off with his crew in tow towards their section. That little nigga had me fucked up, but I wasn't the loose type anyway, so I wasn't worried about him. I had a nigga technically so playing with Akeo wasn't on my list of things to do. Granted he was five minutes close to being non existent, still we were together.

"Isn't that the one who's always giving us a hard time at the job?" Alissea said close to in a hushed tone as if he could hear her.

"Yeah that's his indecisive ass." I said swaying my small hips to the beat.

"He is fine. What are you going to do about Zaire NiNi? You better be careful." Alissea warned.

"Girl I ain't worried bout Zaire or Akeo's ass, they both for everybody and I'm just trying to have some fun anyway. You can't have nothing serious with niggas like that boo." I said assuring her I knew what I was doing.

"Your brother is done." Alissea said laughing at Naseem grinding on a ugly chick on the dance floor.

"I'm recording all this shit for tomorrow." I laughed as we continued to enjoy our night. Every so often I felt eyes on me, but I didn't even acknowledge it, I knew it was Akeo and I wasn't worried or fazed in the least bit. I wouldn't pass judgment on Akeo, but if he knew Naseem and hung with the niggas he did, I'm sure I was right on with my thoughts.

Same Old Shit

Ni'Oni - NiNi

"Who is it?" I yelled at the closed door knowing whoever was on the other side could hear me. Looking through the peephole I didn't see anybody, so I decided to go ahead and open the door; maybe UPS dropped off something.

"What the hell?!" I yelled looking up and down my normally quiet block. I didn't see anything, n type of movement, but in front of me was the shocker. Who the hell leaves a baby in a car seat on someone's porch?

Bending down I saw the prettiest little girl I had ever laid eyes on. Looking at her curly hair that was being tamed by a big yellow headband, down to her slanted grey eyes, pointy little nose and small lips that turned into a wide toothless grin. Tears pooled in my eyes, I'm not sure who birthed this baby girl but I damn sure knew who helped create her.

Picking the car seat up, I brought her in the house going into my living room setting the car seat on the couch I picked her up and placed her in my lap. She was a chunky little thing, but she smelled great, obviously she was well taken care of. Looking in her seat I saw a red piece of paper folded up and picked it up to see what it was. I laid the pretty baby down next to me on the couch putting my leg up as a block, so she wouldn't roll and hit the floor. Unfolding the paper, it read:

Hey Step Mommy! My name is Ziah, my mommy is tired of me being a secret, so she sent me to live with you and my daddy. Inside is any information you will need for me and mommy said to tell my daddy not to look for her.

I hadn't realized I was crying until a few droplets hit the red paper. Looking down I saw a few pieces of paper folded up and looked to see what these could be, one was a social security card the other was a birth certificate, looking over it I saw that Ziah was about six months old and Ziaire had signed her birth certificate. This no-good ass nigga of mine had crossed the line.

I picked up my phone and dialed his number, in typical Zaire fashion it was going straight to voicemail. I tried three more times and got the same result. Ziah started rolling around and talking in baby talk so I laid out one of the fleece blankets I kept on the side of the couch on the floor and laid her on it. I sat and watched her as she flipped on her chubby stomach and started trying to scoot around in an army crawl, if I wasn't dying on the inside I would have been smiling and encouraging her to 'go ahead'.

Hours turned into a day, I still hadn't heard from my nigga and Ziah is still here. I laid her in the other room and I went back to my room to lay down and think about the ways I was going to kill this nigga. Right on time I heard the front door open and close, I sat up in the bed ready for him to hit the threshold of the bedroom. He didn't get an inch in the doorframe before I started firing off on his ass.

"Let me guess, what was it this time; your phone was dead? You didn't have no service? Or wait, wait you lost it and had to buy another one? Which one Zaire? Huh?!" I screamed on my ain't shit sorry ass boyfriend. This nigga thought he was so slick, and I admit at one point he really was. But everything done in the dark comes to the light.

"You need to chill out Ni'Oni damn! I just walked in this muthafucka and I don't feel like hearing your fucking mouth on some real shit!" Zaire's punk ass had the nerve to have an attitude as he walked into the bathroom slamming the door.

"I don't really give a fuck what you feel like! You got some fucking nerve rolling your yellow ass up in here after a day of being M.I. Fuckin A and acting like I'm the problem!" I yelled knowing he could hear me because there wasn't any noise interrupting us. I heard the toilet flush about twenty seconds later and the shower turned on. After being with Zaire for almost six years now I knew his routine like the back of my hand, so I got up and headed to the kitchen. Turning the stove on, I calmly looked for all the material I would need. As I thought about every lonely night, every postponed date night, every prank call, every 'that's our nigga' text, every ratchet ass fight and last but not least the babies; my hands started to shake.

I was at my breaking point and I knew it, pacing in the kitchen I jogged back upstairs to get my phone off the charger. I had to call somebody because the murderous thoughts running through my head right now weren't healthy. I looked at the bleach, salt and pot of water I had placed on the stove start coming to a boil and I knew then that if I didn't get somebody on line one, Zaire would be taking his last breath today in this here house.

"What's up Ni-Baby, I thought you were hibernating?" My very animated best friend answered the phone. Remy and I had been friends since I was seventeen years old, if ever I needed anybody in this world; Remy was the one.

"Bestie," I cried out

"I'm on my way!" Remy yelled

"No! Listen, I'm going to kill him. I swear today is the day. I can't do this anymore." I said pacing back and forth with the phone pressed to my ear.

"Slow down, calm down Ni'Oni. What is going on, did he hit you again? We gone tag team and fuck his bright ass up today, I got time NiNi." Remy dramatically yelled into the phone.

"No. No he didn't touch me, he just got here like ten minutes ago. I'm just so tired man, like why me? Why the fuck he gotta be a dog ass nigga. So I'm on vacation, been on vacation for three days, do you know this is the first time I've seen his bitch ass?! And when he comes in like everything is everything and I fire off on his ass, he tells me he don't feel like hearing my fucking mouth today!" I cried telling my best friend how I was living, it was no secret that my relationship was the shittiest of the shitty, but it still hurt to say it out loud nonetheless.

"So, I decided today would be the last day he would ever have to hear my fucking mouth. I'm about to start this water and add salt and bleach to it, while he's in MY fucking shower washing away his pains I'm going to pour this shit right over his lying, cheating dog ass head!" I was livid, I had been nothing short of an amazing woman to Zaire but he shitted on me every chance he got. I let him slide with the pop up baby mama, I let him slide with the embarrassing trip to the clinic, I even let him slide with the prank phone calls. But after today's new episode of 'Niggas Aint Shit', I'm officially over it.

"Whoa whoa whoa, bestie listen to me baby; he is NOT worth your freedom. He is not worth your sanity, you are my best friend, I love you to death. I'm not sure what he did this time to cause you to snap, but I need you to think smart. I'm out south right now but I will come to you now. Do not do anything that will cause you jail time." Remy pleaded with me. I understood what he was saying but I was pissed to the highest level of pisstivity.

"That's not it though, there's more. I didn't just wake up and get tired today, it wasn't the fact that I couldn't get ahold of him for a day. I was in my own home minding my own damn business and the doorbell rang. I go to open it thinking it might have just been a package or something. It was a package alright but not some shit I ordered; it was a damn baby!" I said face flooded with tears.

"Ni what the fuck you mean a baby? Who's fucking baby?" Remy yelled

"His twin, the little girl looks just like his dog ass, I swear to God. But then the triflin ass mammy leaves a note with the birth certificate and social security card telling me she's tired of being a secret and this was my problem now."

"Ni'Oni, where is the baby?" Remy sounded worried

"In the second room, sleeping. I would never, could never hurt an innocent baby. That daddy on the other hand may not be as lucky. I swear on the grave of my own child, I could kill this nigga today." I started pacing again, I could hear the shower had stopped running so my original plan was out the window.

"Ni'Oni, just listen to me, leave that house now. I will meet you anywhere baby, but you have to get out of there. You aren't in your right state of mind right now and I don't want things to get ugly and I'm not there. Please NiNi!" Remy begged but I wasn't listening to him right now. I want Zaire to hurt the same way I hurt. This was worse than the first time a baby popped up, this was almost as bad when my own sweet angel passed.

"It hurts, why me?" I whispered and cried hanging the phone up. As I looked at the water boiling on the stove, I walked over to it turning the stove off. As I went into the living room I heard the baby start to cry. I hadn't forgot about her, but I didn't think of how I was going to present her to her shitty ass father. I heard him making his way into the second bedroom where Ziah was crying.

"Yo! What the fuck? Ni'Oni!! Baby what's going on?" I heard Zaire say from the top of the stairs. He had apparently picked Ziah up because she was no longer crying, and I could hear her baby gibberish getting closer as he came down the stairs.

I sat in the love seat and waited until he rounded the corner coming in the living room. I know I probably didn't look as bad as I felt but I knew I looked a hot mess regardless. He stood there in the archway and we just stared at each other. I looked at him, look at me and I saw the pain in his eyes. But he had some nerve to be in pain, shit this was all his doing. I didn't go out fucking anything and bringing home std's and babies and crazy bitches; he did. After six long agonizing years, over ten break-ups to makes-ups, two miscarriages, one deceased child, and so many fights, I finally saw that he was sorry. I'd never seen the look he held in his eyes before after all this time, I saw the sorrow.

"Baby let me explain," Zaire started, and I held my hand up to stop him.

"I know, you're so sorry. I know, you didn't mean for this to happen. I know this bitch is lying. I already know what you want to explain Zaire. Save it for me okay?" I was numb, this had taken all the fight out of me.

"Listen, I didn't know how to tell you about her okay? But I swear to God on my soul baby I haven't fucked back with her momma since before she was born" Zaire tried explaining as if that bullshit would make me jump for joy. I typical Zaire fashion he just wanted this to get pushed under the rug and everything to be like it used to be.

"Please, Zaire don't play on my intelligence ok; just don't. I could kill you where you stand right now. I contemplated over fifty ways to end your existence, not even thirty minutes ago you were close to getting a chemical shower. I can't do this anymore, you need to leave. This chapter in our lives is over, it's a wrap."

"So, you just gone be done like that?! That's it huh? Ni'Oni get the fuck out of here with that Maya Angelou shit ma. What's the difference in Ziyah being here than you dealing with my other kids, huh? This aint our first rodeo baby. I know your feelings are hurt, I know a nigga hurt you, I get it you need some space. But don't say this shit is over when we both know it's not." Zaire placed Ziyah on the floor after his little speech and started walking towards me. I took two steps backwards.

"See that right there, what you just said is the problem. True enough this isn't our first rodeo as you say. But it is the final rodeo. Get whatever you can now and get out. Whatever is left, I'll drop it by your mama's house." I walked away heading to my other bedroom turned office space. I heard Zaire calling out to me but when Ziyah started to whine he turned his attention to her and off me. I heard him go up the stairs with her and I plopped down on the chase style chair in the room.

I couldn't cry anymore, I was standing by what I had said rather he believed it or not. This toxic shit Zaire and I had dragged on all these years was over and done with today. As I closed my eyes I heard my phone chime with a text. I picked it up and saw an unsaved number had text me asking what I was doing. I waited about three minutes and I had gotten a text back, out of the days and times, this nigga text me now. What was the irony in that? Looking at my phone again, I decided to save the number and text back.

Akeo.

If you would like to stay updated on future releases, discussions or just want to get to know Jaii Lynn here's how you can;

Facebook – Lady-Jai Lynnette

Instagram - _muva.jaii_

Facebook Author Page – Jaii Lynn The Authoress

Made in the USA
Columbia, SC
09 October 2018